FLYAWAY

BY HELEN LANDALF

HARCOURT

Houghton Mifflin Harcourt
Boston New York 2011

Harcourt is an imprint of Houghton Mifflin Harcourt Publishing Company.

www.hmhbooks.com

Text set in Garamond.

Library of Congress Cataloging-in-Publication Data
Landalf, Helen.
Flyaway / by Helen Landalf.
p. cm.
Summary: Seattle fifteen-year-old Stevie Calhoun does not realize how bad her life is until her mother leaves and Stevie must move in with annoyingly perfect Aunt Mindy for a summer, filling her days with being tutored and volunteering at a bird rehabilitation center.
ISBN 978-0-547-51973-9
[1. Family problems—Fiction. 2. Interpersonal relations—Fiction. 3. Birds—Protection—Fiction. 4. Wildlife rescue—Fiction. 5. Family life—Washington (State)—Seattle—Fiction. 6. Drug abuse—Fiction. 7. Seattle (Wash.)—Fiction.] I. Title.
PZ7.L231655Fly 2011
[Fic]—dc22
2011009592

Manufactured in the United States of America
DOC 10 9 8 7 6 5 4 3 2 1
4500329200

For my mother, Gloria Rimland,
for many years of loving support

Just when I'm starting to think she might be dead or something, the phone rings. I lunge for it, banging my shin on the coffee table and sending Mom's ashtray tumbling to the floor. Ashes scatter on the burnt-orange carpet.

"Mom?"

No answer.

"Mom?" I say again.

"Hello, there." It's a man's voice, low and fakey-smooth. At first I'm scared it's Drake. Then he says, "I'm calling from Rainier Collection Services. Is this Ms. J. Calhoun?"

I put on my politest voice. "Sorry, you must have the wrong number." Then I set the receiver down with a *click* and remind myself for the zillionth time not to answer without checking the caller ID. Sinking onto the couch, I study the new bruise on my shin, just above the ankle bracelet Mom made me for my birthday last year. I don't know what I'm getting myself so worked up for. Mom has had to work late plenty of times.

I close my eyes and listen. It's almost eleven, and the only sounds are the *thunk* our kitchen clock makes and the *swoosh* of cars hydroplaning through the lake-size puddle in the street outside. I keep waiting for one of those cars to stop and Mom to come swooping into the apartment with her jasmine-and-cigarette smell and her "Hey, honey pie, you still awake?" and her big, husky laugh. But the cars just roll on by.

I'm kind of wishing the Professor would call, take my mind off

Mom. A couple of weeks ago he called while Mom was at work, and we argued for like an hour about whether other people really exist or we just make them up in our heads. He thinks we create the whole world in our minds. I say that's a load of crap, because why would we create a bunch of wars and pollution? He may be the smartest kid at Ballard High, but that doesn't mean he's right about everything. It's probably too late for him to call tonight, though. He's got school tomorrow.

The quiet in the apartment is starting to creep me out, so I fish the remote from between the couch cushions and turn on the TV. A *Family Guy* rerun is on the only channel we get, and I've seen it like fifty million times. Characters from another show float across the screen like ghosts. I turn it off.

Thunk, says the kitchen clock.

The phone rings again, and this time I remember to check the caller ID. *Calhoun, M.* Mom's sister, Mindy. Miss Perfect. Like her house, for example. Perfect white couch, perfect polished wood floor, perfect matching wine glasses. She acts like just because we live in an apartment, we're a couple of lowlifes. No way am I picking up for her.

When the phone stops ringing, I punch in the number for Mom's work.

Her boss answers, but I can hardly hear him over the voices and loud music in the background. Wednesday is No-Cover Night at the club; the place is probably packed.

"Hi, Alex. It's me again."

"Hey, Stevie-girl. I already told you, your mom's off tonight."

"I thought she might—"

"Sorry, haven't seen her since yesterday morning." He clicks his tongue. "What's she doing, leaving you all alone like that?"

I force a laugh. "Hey, I'm fifteen, remember? I can take care of myself."

"Still, that's awful young for—"

"Oh, here she is right now. Hi, Mom!" I call toward the front door.

"Let me talk—"

I hang up before he can finish.

Thunk, says the clock.

There is one other place Mom could be. When I grit my teeth and press the button on the caller ID a couple of times, sure enough, the name comes up: *Uttley, Drake.*

I've only ever met him once, but even seeing his name makes my throat go dry. The corn dog and fries I ate for dinner start kicking around in my stomach. Someone shouts out in the street, so I shut the window. But that makes me feel more sweaty, more closed in, so I open it again. I try to make myself pick up the phone and call Drake's number to see if Mom's there, but I can't. I just can't.

The phone rings again. Aunt Mindy. What does she keep calling for? It's not like she and Mom are best buddies or anything. She's only ever been over once that I know of, and that was only to drop off a check. Another time, she lied about us to Child Protective Services, tried to get them to take me away. CPS. They go after parents who tie their kids up in the basement and feed them moldy bread. Still, what if it's important? What if it's something about Mom? I reach for the phone, but my heart's beating so fast I can hardly breathe. I change my mind and let it ring.

All these calls are making me jittery, so I turn on the TV again. There's an even louder shout outside and then the sound of breaking glass. Every *thunk* of the kitchen clock makes me worry more about Mom.

Finally I can't sit still another second, so I decide to clean the apartment and surprise her when she gets home. After I shove the stack of bills inside the drawer of the coffee table and arrange the cushions so they hide the purple wine stain on the couch, I find the vacuum wedged behind some boxes at the back of Mom's bedroom closet and plug it in.

It won't turn on. I kick it twice, the second time so hard I chip the black polish off my big toenail. That doesn't do anything but make my toe throb. When I plug it into a different outlet, it makes a noise like a jet plane taking off, but at least it runs. I go over every inch of the apartment. It takes me forever.

But I can't get rid of Mom's ashes. I rub and rub and rub at them so hard with the vacuum, I'm surprised I don't tear the carpet. I get down on my knees and try to scrape them up with my fingernails, but all that does is spread them around and make the tips of my fingers raw. When I sit up and wipe my cheek, I'm surprised to find it's damp.

I'm just about to give up and put away the vacuum when there's a knock at the front door. I freeze.

"Stevie?" someone calls. "It's me, sweetie!"

The voice is so much like Mom's that I rush to the door. Then it hits me who the voice belongs to.

I crack it open, and sure enough, there's Aunt Mindy.

CHAPTER 2

Aunt Mindy shoves her way into the apartment and throws herself at me. Her plum-colored exercise outfit—leggings with matching top—is slippery against my bare skin, and she smells like some kind of tropical fruit.

"You didn't answer my calls," she says. "I was getting worried."

I wiggle out of her grasp. "I was in the shower. What are you doing here, anyway?"

She takes one look at my face and says, "Oh, sweetheart, you've been crying."

I swipe at my eyes. "Allergies."

I'd forgotten how much Aunt Mindy looks like Mom. Same curly dark hair, olive-colored skin, and sharp nose as all of us Calhouns. But even though Aunt Mindy is taller than Mom, her hair and body are tight and trim instead of spilling over like foam from a mug of beer. I can't figure out what she's doing here, but I'm pretty sure it can't be good.

"Did something happen to Mom?" I ask.

She pushes past me and scans the living room. "I take it she's not here."

"She's at work."

"I called the club. They said she hasn't been in since yesterday morning." She shakes her head. "Classic June, leaving you alone this time of night."

I frown at her. "Why are you bugging her at work?"

She looks me up and down, like she's checking out my outfit: a pair of red and black men's boxers I picked up at the thrift store and a teeny pink Hello Kitty tank. Mom says I've got style, but obviously, Aunt Mindy doesn't get it. I'm hoping she doesn't notice the messed-up polish on my big toenail.

She puts her hands on her nonexistent hips. "You're looking thin. Are you getting enough to eat?"

I roll my eyes. This is so Aunt Mindy, sticking her big fat nose in our business.

Her leggings make a swishing sound as she bustles into the kitchen. It's embarrassing, the way they're so tight you can see the outline of her butt. She pulls open the fridge, peers inside, and shakes her head. "I bet you haven't had a bite of dinner."

"I had a corn dog."

She gets this look on her face like I just told her I ate bug snot. "A *corn dog*? Oh, honey, isn't she feeding you any vegetables?"

"I got it at the 7-Eleven. And it came with fries." Like it's any of her business.

"I don't believe it. She has you eating dinner at 7-Eleven while she runs around all hours of the night."

She heads for the living room, and I'm sure she's about to pick up the phone and call CPS.

I'm right behind her. "Don't."

"Don't what?" She stops, and her dark eyes narrow. "Where is she, Stevie?"

I shrug and stare at my mutant toenail.

"Come on. I know something's going on here. I heard some disturbing news today about that . . . *place* she works at. I was hoping it wasn't true, but—"

"What disturbing news?"

She grabs my hand. "Tell me the truth, Stevie. Has she been acting different lately? Has she been spending long periods away from home? Have strange people been calling here?"

"No!" I jerk my hand away. "I don't know what you're talking about."

"When did you last see her?"

I cross my arms over my chest.

She glances toward the phone. I can't take the chance she might actually pick it up.

"Yesterday. I saw her yesterday morning."

Her hand flies to her mouth. "You've been alone here for two days?"

I'm not about to tell her, but it's actually been three. Leave it to Aunt Mindy to make a federal case out of nothing. "It's not a big deal. I'm totally used to it."

She moves toward the phone, and I'm ready to tackle her if she tries to pick it up. But she passes it to finger the dried-up leaves of the plant on the windowsill. "Poor little hydrangea. I bet no one's watered you in ages."

She's right about that. Some neighbor lady gave the plant to Mom about a month ago. It's kind of weird-looking, with these little flowers bunched into round clusters that look like blue popcorn balls nestled in the green leaves. Mom stuck it by the window. I don't think she's looked at it since.

"It's just a plant," I say.

She looks at the plant and then at me. Her lips get so thin they pretty much disappear. "I'm getting you out of here, Stevie."

"No way. I'm not going anywhere."

"Either you come with me, or I'll have to start making some calls. Now go pack your stuff."

I stare at her, trying to figure out if she'll really do it. Mom's told me a hundred times that Mindy loves to mess with your mind. Still, I can't take any chances.

"What if Mom comes back and finds me gone?"

"Leave her a note." She fishes through her purse and hands me a pen.

I glare at her and pull an envelope from under the coffee table. *Mom,* I scrawl on the back, *At Mindy's.* I sign it *S.*

"Fine," I say as I slap the note next to Mom's ashtray. "I'll spend the night at your place. But I'm not packing anything, because I'm coming right back here tomorrow."

She lifts the plant off the windowsill. I swear she's got tears in her eyes. How lame can you get, crying over a stupid plant?

"Actually," she says, "I wouldn't count on that."

"Get up, Stevie," a voice says way too early the next morning.

For a second I'm not sure where I am. But when I open my eyes and see Aunt Mindy standing over me with an "I Love Pilates" coffee mug in her hand, it all comes crashing back. I also realize why I slept so well. The bed in her guest room is big and soft, not lumpy like the one I usually sleep on. Still, I'd give anything to be in my own bed right now.

She moves in close, and I can smell coffee on her breath. "Come on, lazybones. I've got a mat class at eight."

Aunt Mindy owns a Pilates studio, which, as far as me and Mom can tell, is where a bunch of rich ladies go to tighten their butts. "Have fun," I mumble, and then pull the blankets over my head.

She pulls them right back off. "I'm going to drop you at school on my way."

School. The word hits me with a hollow thump, like the thud a rock makes when you drop it in a deep hole. "Can't go to school," I say. I'm too foggy to be creative, so I go for the oldest excuse in the book. "Don't feel good."

She presses the back of her hand against my forehead. "You feel okay to me."

I pinch my thigh hard to make my eyes tear up. "Please, not today."

This time her voice is softer. "You're stressed about your mom, aren't you? Tell you what, you stay home and rest. I'll give school a call."

Call school? *Mayday, we have a problem here.* I sit up. "You don't have to call. I just need to bring a note when I go back."

She frowns. "Is that so?" Then she glances at her watch. "Look, kiddo, I've really got to run. There's stuff in the fridge if you're hungry. I've got some DVDs in the cabinet under the TV, and you're welcome to root through my library. I'll bring us home something for dinner. You like Chinese?"

I shrug.

"I'm interviewing a new instructor at five, so I'll probably be home about six-thirty. And don't worry about your mom, Stevie. Let me handle that."

She finally leaves me alone, and a few minutes later I hear her take off out the front door. The silence that blankets the house is almost as cozy as the yellow checkered quilt that covers me. In spite of myself, I relax into it. For once I don't have to listen for the phone. I sigh and let myself drift off to sleep again.

When I wake up it's after eleven, and I've got a caffeine-withdrawal headache from hell. I hustle into the kitchen and pour myself what's left in the coffeemaker, but it's so bitter I have to spit it out in the sink. The plant from our apartment sits on the kitchen counter with water droplets on its leaves. Which kind of pisses me off. That plant was Mom's. So what if she forgot to water it?

After I rinse the coffee mug and fill it with water from the tap, I stand back and check out Aunt Mindy's kitchen. Disgustingly perfect, of course. Lacy curtains flutter in the windows, and the sun reflecting on the yellow table makes it look like a pool of melted butter. I pull the curtains aside and see her perfect backyard. Thick green bushes dotted with pink flowers line the fence, and a pine tree towers in one corner.

With Aunt Mindy gone, I decide it's time to do a little snooping around. I carry my mug of water into the dining room, where I run my hands along the smooth, polished wood of the table and open the cabinets to check out her fine china. I already know the bathroom's got a huge tub and a tile shower with sliding glass doors, but I had no idea Aunt Mindy had a flat-screen TV in her bedroom. With a TV like that, I can't figure out why she has like five thousand books. I end my tour in the living room, with its fancy piano, which I'll bet no one's ever played, and an L-shaped white couch. *Big bucks* is what I'm thinking.

Me and Mom do this thing when we're bored where we imagine the house we're going to buy once she gets enough money to get her jewelry business going and we don't have to live in apartments anymore. It's got a bedroom for each of us, a bathroom like Aunt Mindy's with a shower *and* a tub, and a living room even cooler than this one. We call it our NTD House. NTD stands for not too distant, as in Mom's making some killer business connections right now, so we're going to have a house like that in the not-too-distant future. Oh, and it's got a nice wide front porch where Mom can go for a smoke.

I picture Mom kicking back on a porch swing, blowing smoke

out the side of her mouth the way she does, and suddenly I need to talk to her so bad it hurts. I dial our number on Aunt Mindy's phone, but it just rings. I hang up before the answering machine kicks in. You never know with Mom. Sometimes she likes to lie in bed, enjoy her cigarette, and ignore the phone.

I scarf down a bowl of cereal and throw on some clothes. I know Aunt Mindy wouldn't like it, but I've got to go back to the apartment. I've got to see if Mom is there.

It's a little cool for the beginning of June, so I go through my bag and find a long-sleeved gas-station-attendant's shirt to wear over my halter top, and thick socks for under my used Doc Martens. Aunt Mindy never gave me a key, so I have to leave the door unlocked. I'll be back way before she comes home, anyway. I catch the number 71 bus downtown and then transfer to the 48, which will take me to the Ballard neighborhood.

It's a long ride, but I don't mind. I've been riding Metro ever since we moved to Seattle last summer, so I'm pretty used to it. Of course, if I had a car, I could get around a lot faster. I've been bugging Mom for months to let me get a learner's permit, but whenever I bring it up she just blows air through her lips and says, "What do you need that for? You already know how to drive." It's true, back in Montana she'd let me take the wheel if she'd had too many beers, as long as we were off the highway and there weren't any cops around. But I doubt that's the kind of practice the driver's license people have in mind.

As the bus gets closer to our neighborhood, the houses turn into dumpy apartments. I get off at 8th and 85th and head toward our street.

After passing the Four Spoons Cafe, I hang a right on 9th and take the shortcut through the cemetery. Most people think cemeteries are creepy, but I think they're cool. I like to imagine those dead people hanging out under the grass, talking about what goes on up here. Who knows, maybe they're watching out for me.

I turn onto the skinny street that borders the west end of the cemetery and pass the place I call Crow House because the old lady who lives there always sits on the porch in her bathrobe and talks to the crows. She's not in her usual spot today, but there are plenty of crows around. A fat one perches on the telephone wire and caws at me. It sounds so sassy I put my hands on my hips and caw right back.

Chirp! From behind me comes a high-pitched cry that's definitely not a crow's. I turn my head in the direction of the sound, but all I see are the blackberry bushes growing over the cemetery fence. *Chirp!* This time I look down. A baby bird with only a few scruffy feathers staggers in the dirt near my feet. It wobbles, then flails its wings and falls over.

I kneel beside the bird. "Don't worry. I'm not going to hurt you."

It trembles and chirps even louder.

There's no way this bird is going to survive on its own. It's so small and helpless and so close to the road, I know it's just a matter of time before it gets flattened by a car or mauled by a cat. I inch closer and hold out my hands. "It's okay. I'll take care of you."

"Hey! Don't touch that robin!" The guy's voice is a low growl.

I turn. I didn't notice the silver Honda parked across the street before, but now I see a guy about my age staring at me through the open driver's side window. Glossy dark hair falls across his forehead and frames his angry jaw. With that voice, he makes me think of a pissed-off grizzly bear in sunglasses.

"This bird is lost or something," I tell him.

"What do you know about birds?"

Wait. I know that growl. I study the guy more closely and realize I also know that face. And those sunglasses.

It's all coming back. Alan Parker got expelled back in October for spray-painting "Jeff Taylor is a faggot" in big black letters on the front of the school. Even before that, he had a reputation as the meanest kid at Ballard High. He was the guy who tripped the special ed kids and made them fall on their faces. The guy who wrote an essay for the school paper calling the rest of us "sheep." Some girls thought he was hot, but when I look at him, all I see is a world-class loser.

"Hey, did you hear me?" he calls.

I don't answer.

He looks me up and down and smirks. "I remember you. Ballard High. I heard your mom's a babe. Keep meaning to go downtown and check out her act one of these days."

I'm used to kids saying stuff like that, so I pretend not to hear.

"You're Stephanie, right?"

"Stevie." I'm careful to keep any hint of friendliness out of my voice.

He nods toward my feet, where the bird sits huddled in the dirt, trembling. "Now, get away from that bird."

"I'm going to take it home . . . I mean, to my aunt's."

He swings open the car door, unfolds his body from the seat, and then saunters across the street like he owns it. His faded jeans hug his thighs, and from the way he fills out his green army jacket, I can tell he's been working out.

"Look, Stephanie—"

"Stevie."

"Stevie. You don't know what to feed this bird or how often it needs to eat. I bet you were going to give it a cute little name, weren't you?"

I hadn't thought about the feeding thing. But I was thinking of calling her Tweety Bird, after my favorite cartoon character.

"What makes you the bird expert?"

"I work at a bird rehab clinic, okay? Someone put in a call about this robin, and I've been observing it for the past hour. By the way, you don't just pick up a baby bird without waiting to see if its parents are around. A mother bird always comes back for her babies, unless she's hurt. Or dead." He tilts his head, and the sun glints off his dark lenses. I hate not being able to see his eyes. "The clinic's got incubators, aviaries, the works. Which I assume you don't."

He's making me feel like such a moron I want to punch him in the nose, and I can't imagine why any bird clinic would hire a reject like him. But I have to admit, it sounds like he's a lot more set up to help the bird than I am.

"Fine. Take it, then."

He moves toward the bird and wraps one hand around it with a quick motion so the bird's head sticks out between two of his fingers. He holds it toward me. "Only safe way to pick up a bird."

Big friggin' deal, I feel like saying. "What's wrong with giving a bird a name?" I ask instead.

He motions me to follow him across the street to his car. He opens up the passenger side and then nods toward the back seat. "Open that box."

Even though I hate him bossing me around, I lift the lid off the shoebox that sits on the torn vinyl seat. Inside is one of those green plastic baskets strawberries come in, filled with wadded-up toilet paper. He sets the bird on the toilet paper, and I realize it's a nest.

"You don't want to get attached to a wild bird," he says as he slips the lid back on the shoebox. The bird chirps inside. "You name it, you'll have a hard time letting it go. Well, I'm going to get this bird over to the clinic." He smirks at me. "Sorry to steal your pet."

He gets in the car and turns on the engine. I kick the ground, making a brown gash in the grass. As I head back to the other side of the street, I call, "Her name's Tweety Bird!"

He sticks his arm out the window and tosses a card at me. "Come by the clinic sometime. You might learn something," he says. Then he peels away.

I watch till his car disappears before I pick up the card. *On the Wing: Bird Rehabilitation,* it says in small black letters. *Valerie Harrison, licensed wildlife rehabilitator.* It lists an address and a phone number, which I barely look at. I shove the card in my pocket and head toward the apartment. Just the thought that Mom might be there makes me walk faster.

Our apartment is in a little complex across the street from a McDonald's and a Chevron station.

A couple of guys stand out front, staring under the open hood of a truck. "I told you the choke's shot," one of them says as I walk by. Then he tosses a cigarette butt into the street. They smell like beer.

Each unit has its own number painted on the front door. Ours is number 11. I check out our window. The blinds are partway open. I don't remember if they were like that when I left, but I hurry to the door and fumble with my keys. "Mom," I call. I can't get the door unlocked quick enough.

The orange shag carpet glares at me, and the vacuum's still parked in the middle of the living room. My note to Mom sits next to her ashtray, exactly where I left it.

I slump onto the couch and stare at the water stain on the ceiling, the one that always reminds me of a spider. Then I notice the answering machine is blinking. There are a couple of calls from Alex, wondering why Mom hasn't made it in to work. *Delete.* Then a call from Mrs. Watkins, my counselor at Ballard High: "Ms. Calhoun, we need to discuss Stevie's attendance, blah, blah, blah . . . *Delete.*

And then Tonya's voice comes blaring out at me: "Stevie, it's me. Guess what? Mike's going out of town. You know what that means, so call me back, okay? And get yourself a cell already."

Yes, I know what that means: Tonya and her caveman brother, Doug, are throwing another drunken party. Last time he barfed all over the back deck. No, thanks. *Delete.*

I move away from the phone and notice a couple of unopened bills lying on the floor below the mail slot, including one stamped "Past Due" in big red letters. Whenever Mom starts getting bills like that, it's not long before we have to find a new place to live.

I'm about to leave when I notice Mom's bedroom door is shut. I'm positive I left it open when I went in to get the vacuum. I stand there not knowing what to do. If she's asleep, the last thing I want to do is wake her up. And if she's awake, she might not be in the mood for a visitor.

But then again, I'm sure she'd want to see me. She might even perk up and say, "Well, there you are, honey pie. Come give your old mom a hug."

I knock on the door. "Mom?" There's no answer, so I crack it open.

The room is dark and empty, but the covers on Mom's bed are rumpled. I lay my cheek against her pillow and breathe in her scent. She's been here; at least I know she's alive.

Then I notice the drawer of the little table by her bed is open. I slide it out a hair further. The dog-eared envelope where she stashes the grocery money sits on top of her lacy bras and panties. It's empty.

I get this sick feeling in the pit of my stomach, and I just know I have to check. I go into my bedroom and feel under the bed till I find the heart-shaped metal box where I keep my treasures: a reddish rock from Grandpa's ranch in Montana, a shell I found on the beach in Carkeek Park, a bird's egg wrapped in cotton. And my money. I had forty-five dollars I'd saved up from babysitting in there. Now it's gone. Not only that, the egg is broken and the inside of the box is coated with yellow slime.

For a second I'm so pissed I want to slam the box against the wall. But only for a second. Mom never takes my money unless there's a good reason, like that time she borrowed fifty bucks to cover rent. She probably needed it for one of those bills, and she'll pay me right back as soon as she gets her check. Or maybe they accepted her application to sell jewelry at the street fair, and she needed it to pay for a booth or something. It's me I should be pissed at, blaming Mom when all she's trying to do is make things better for us. Still the sick feeling won't leave me, and I wish my money was still there.

I rinse out the box in the bathroom sink, tuck it under my arm, and slip out the front door, locking it behind me. It's gotten even cooler outside, and the two guys are still poking around under the hood of the truck. I sprint to the bus stop just in time to catch the number 48. I make the transfer downtown, but I'm working so hard to come up with other reasons my money might be gone, I miss the stop in Wedgewood and have to walk five blocks back to Aunt Mindy's.

She wasn't supposed to be home till six-thirty. But here it is, the middle of the afternoon, and her spotless white Camry is parked in the driveway.

CHAPTER **4**

Aunt Mindy is waiting for me on the living room couch with her arms crossed and her mouth pressed into a thin line. She's changed out of her workout gear into a pair of designer jeans and a tight blue T-shirt. The heat's cranked up to about ninety degrees, and little half-moons of sweat peek from under her arms.

"Hi," I say over my shoulder, as I head for the guest room, trying to sound cool and casual.

"Stop right there. Where have you been?"

"Where do you think? School."

She crosses her arms over her chest. "School."

"I was feeling better, so I took the bus."

"That's interesting, because your counselor says you haven't been to school all week."

I swallow. I feel like I'm perched at the top of a roller coaster, about to drop.

"And here I rescheduled my interview so I could pick up your homework."

Pick up my homework? Who does she think she is, my mom? I start to walk away, but she stands and comes after me.

"June lets you get away with this, doesn't she? She lets you cut school."

"And your point is . . . ?"

"And I see she lets you mouth off too."

"Whatever."

She grabs my shoulder. "Don't 'whatever' me. And by the way, you went off and left the door unlocked."

I jerk away so hard I jab her with my elbow. "Get your friggin' hands off me!"

"Hey, watch it! If you were my kid—"

"Well, I'm not! And quit blaming everything on Mom!" I storm into the guest room, slam the door behind me, and throw myself face-down on the bed. For a minute it's quiet. Then I hear the *tap, tap* of Aunt Mindy's sandals approaching the door.

"Stevie?"

I bury my face in the checkered quilt.

"Stevie, can I come in?"

"Shut up!" I snatch the vanilla-scented candle from the little table by the bed and hurl it at the door. It hits with a *thump.*

"Stevie, please."

I don't answer, and pretty soon her footsteps click off into the distance. About ten minutes later, the front door slams.

The quiet in the house isn't cozy anymore—it suffocates me. I lie there with my fists clenched and stare at the ceiling. I should just get out of here, go stay at the apartment. But no doubt she'd find me and drag me back. I decide the only way I'm going to get through this is to keep my mouth shut as much as possible.

When there's a knock on the door maybe half an hour later, I open up to see Aunt Mindy standing there in sweats and running shoes, damp curls plastered to her forehead.

"I went for a run," she says. "Always makes me feel better."

I keep my face blank.

"I'm starving. There's a great little Chinese place on Fifteenth.

How does that sound?"

I'd kill right now for a corn dog, but whatever. "Sounds okay."

"Great," she says. "I'll hop in the shower."

The restaurant she picks is crowded and dark and stinks of incense. The hostess smiles at Aunt Mindy and shows us to a table in the back.

"This is one of my favorite places," Aunt Mindy says. "I usually come here alone, so it's nice to have company."

I stare at the weird names on the menu: Moo Shu this and Goo Goo that. "What is this stuff?"

She laughs. "I bet you haven't had much Chinese. Your mom's always been a burgers-and-fries kind of gal."

What's wrong with burgers and fries? I think. But I stick to my plan and stay quiet.

The waitress slides a pot of tea onto the table between us and turns over our cups. They look like miniature white cereal bowls.

Aunt Mindy pours herself some tea. "I remember one time, way before you were born, I took your mom to a little Chinese place that had just opened up in Helena. She stared at the menu like you're doing, with her forehead all wrinkled up. When the waitress came to take our order, June said, 'I'll have the Egg Foo Yung.' But when the food arrived, she took one look at it and said, 'What is this crap? I thought I ordered eggs.'" Aunt Mindy chuckles and shakes her head. "She expected it to be a plate of eggs and hash browns, like in some diner."

If we weren't in a restaurant, I'd throw the pot of tea at her. So Mom isn't all cultured and sophisticated. She's still worth a million Aunt Mindys.

The waitress comes to take our order.

"You should try the Kung Pao Chicken," Aunt Mindy says.

I mentally stick out my tongue at her, then I turn to the waitress. "Give me the Egg Foo Yung."

When I finally give up on chopsticks and ask the waitress for a fork, I can see why Mom was surprised. Egg Foo Yung tastes nothing like eggs. It's actually pretty good—these spongy, spicy little pancake things with yummy brown sauce all over them. I start to wish I hadn't worn my tight jeans.

I'm hoping we can eat in peace, but no. Aunt Mindy has to tell me stories about when she and Mom were girls, back on Grandpa's ranch in Montana. She makes a big deal about all the times she saved Mom's butt when they were kids. "I spent so much time keeping June out of trouble, you'd have thought I was her mom instead of her little sister," she says.

I've got half a mind to get up and leave, when all of a sudden she gets quiet. "Stevie," she says, "I owe you an apology for what I said back at the house. I never should have criticized your mom."

I pick up one of the chopsticks and poke at the pool of sauce on my plate. I wonder what she's up to now.

"We've always had different ideas about raising you. But you're not my daughter, so I had no right to say what I did."

I use the chopstick to paint pictures: a heart, a bird, a tree.

"Truth is, I love your mom. If I get mad at her sometimes, it's just because I worry about her. She never quite seems to get her life off the ground."

I knew it. I knew she couldn't say something nice about Mom without twisting it around. I grip the chopstick so hard I'm surprised it doesn't break.

The waitress brings the check and a couple of fortune cookies, but Aunt Mindy doesn't seem to notice. She locks her eyes on mine and says, "You need to get back to school, Stevie. If you screw up high school, you'll be crippled before you even start your life. I don't want to see you end up . . . having regrets."

I know exactly what she's thinking. She doesn't want me to end up like Mom.

"I made an appointment for us to see your school counselor tomorrow. We'll talk to her together, okay?"

I let the chopstick clatter onto the plate. "Forget it."

"I'm afraid it's settled. Mrs. Watkins is concerned about your future, and so am I."

"I'm not going to—"

"Unless you want me to bring CPS into this."

Sometimes I want to strangle her. "Fine. I'll talk to her."

"Good." She smiles. She just loves getting her way.

She picks up the check and starts rummaging in her purse. "There's something else I wanted to talk to you about. While you're staying with me, I expect you to pitch in around the house. This weekend we'll make a list of chores you can be responsible for."

I'm used to doing housework. Mom's busy a lot, so I end up doing most of the cleaning. I don't really mind it, but I'm not about to tell Aunt Mindy that. "No way," I whine.

"Yes, way. But the news isn't all bad. I'm also going to start giving you an allowance. How does twenty dollars a week sound?"

It sounds like the most money anyone's handed me for doing pretty much nothing, but that's another thing Aunt Mindy doesn't need to know. "Sounds all right," I say with a shrug.

"And I'm going to put you on my cell phone plan. With me

working all the time, we'll need a way to stay in touch. Maybe we can pick out a phone for you this weekend."

Me and Mom hate cell phones. Every time we see someone jabbering on one, we pinch our noses in the universal PU sign and bust out laughing. But if Aunt Mindy's dumb enough to buy me one, sure, I'll take it.

"Now let's see what the future has in store for us." She sets her credit card on the little plastic tray and picks up a fortune cookie. "Me first." She cracks it open and reads: "You will soon have everything you dream of."

She laughs and rolls her eyes, and for a second she looks exactly like Mom. "That'll be the day. Now your turn."

The fortune cookie is light and fragile as a bird's egg. It cracks open easily. I read the fortune to myself: *The love you seek is right in front of you.*

Aunt Mindy leans forward. "What's it say?"

I stuff the fortune in my pocket. "It says I'm going to win a million dollars."

I toss and turn all night thinking about the meeting with Mrs. Watkins. But when six-thirty the next morning rolls around and Aunt Mindy turns on the shower, I know there's no way out.

"You didn't have to dress up just for me," she says as she grabs her car keys off the hook near the front door. She looks all sharp in jeans and a jacket and little gold hoop earrings. Her curls are stiff with some kind of gel. I've got on black high-tops, black jeans with holes in the knees, and a black T-shirt. "You look like you're dressed for a funeral."

Exactly.

Mrs. Watkins's office is on the second floor. The room is so tiny she looks like a walrus in a goldfish bowl.

"Hello again," she says to Aunt Mindy. Then she turns to me. "Hey, stranger. Long time no see."

I can't look at her, so I keep my eyes on her huge belly, which pooches over the waistband of her pants. Everyone at Ballard High knows Mrs. Watkins may look all soft and squishy, but she never takes "no" for an answer, and if you even think about trying to scam her, you're screwed.

She moves the stacks of papers that bury a couple of folding chairs. "Please sit down, you two. It's definitely time we had a talk." She perches on the edge of her desk, and her thighs spread like pancake batter in a pan. Not pretty.

"I'm so glad you stopped in yesterday," she tells Aunt Mindy. "I've left a number of messages with Stevie's mom, but she hasn't returned my calls."

"Yes, well, that doesn't surprise me."

Mrs. Watkins turns her stun-gun eyes on me. "So, Stevie, you didn't show up for any of your classes this week, and you had an unexcused absence last week as well. What's up?"

I was awake all night figuring out ways to answer this, but I'm too nervous to remember any of them. "I couldn't make it, that's all."

Aunt Mindy glares at me. "You know that's no excuse—"

"Let's let Stevie speak for herself." Mrs. Watkins leans toward me. "We want to help you, Stevie. Can you tell us why you haven't been coming to school?"

The room is stuffy, and Mrs. Watkins gives off a stale, oniony smell. I'm starting to sweat.

"I . . . my mom needed me to help out at home." I sneak a peek at

Aunt Mindy. I can see the wheels turning, but she doesn't say anything.

"Go on," Mrs. Watkins says. "You were helping your mom."

I wriggle in my seat like a fish on a hook, but Mrs. Watkins's eyes hold me in a vise grip. The image of my heart-shaped box swims before my eyes, and all of a sudden the truth comes blurting out: "I stayed home to answer the phone."

The second it's out of my mouth, I know I've blown it bigtime. Mrs. Watkins looks confused, but Aunt Mindy practically leaps out of her seat.

"I knew it. June's got you caught up in this crystal thing, doesn't she?"

Mrs. Watkins frowns. "Crystal thing?"

I'm hyperventilating and I feel like I'm ready to pass out.

"A client of mine told me about it," Aunt Mindy says. "Her brother's a cop." She glances at me, then turns back to Mrs. Watkins. "This nightclub Stevie's mom works at? Apparently it's a front for dealing crystal meth."

I jump up and kick at my chair. "Liar!" Then I barrel toward the door.

Mrs. Watkins grabs my shoulder. With a hold like that, I'm thinking she should get a second job as a bouncer.

"Hang on a minute," she says. "Let's talk this thing through. I wonder if you're aware of school board attendance policy. Seven unexcused absences in a calendar month, and you've got a date in truancy court."

I freeze. Court? I try to count up the days I've been absent in my head, but I've lost track.

She dumps me back in the chair. "So you were saying you stayed home to answer the phone. Tell us more about that."

I'm not about to tell her that staying at home to look after Mom was my idea, that I'm scared she'll crash so hard she'll sleep right through those calls. Or the smoke detector going off. Or the landlord pounding on the door, swearing about the rent.

I'm sweating so bad, I wonder if I forgot to wear deodorant. "My mom's trying to get this business thing going, okay? She's trying to get together enough money to start her own jewelry company. She designs really cool beads and earrings and stuff." I see Aunt Mindy roll her eyes. I know I'm talking way too fast, but it's out of my control. "She has to sleep during the day, and I just wanted to make sure she didn't miss any important calls."

"And this has nothing to do with this situation your aunt's talking about?"

"No!"

Now Aunt Mindy's out of her chair. "My sister can't even keep her life together. How's she going to run a jewelry business? When I went over the other night to check on Stevie, there wasn't a scrap of food in the house. She hadn't seen her mom in two days. That was two days ago, and we still haven't heard from her."

Mrs. Watkins looks at me. "Is that true, Stevie?"

I stare at the floor. My heart's pounding a million miles an hour.

"I can understand your concern about the drugs," she tells Aunt Mindy, "but at this point, that's hearsay. Let's deal with what we've got in front of us. I assume Stevie's safe at the moment?"

Aunt Mindy sinks back into her chair. "She's staying with me now."

The way she says "now" makes it sound like "forever."

"And you do realize I'm obligated by law to report any possible instance of neglect to CPS," Mrs. Watkins says.

Okay, I'm officially screwed. I slump in my chair and hide my face in my hands.

"You and I can discuss that later," I hear Mrs. Watkins tell Aunt Mindy. "For now, let's talk about our next step here. We need to get Stevie back on track."

I keep my face buried in my hands. What's the point in going back to classes now? It's all just parties and end-of-the-year stuff anyway. I want to tell them I can't think about school when Mom's not paying the bills and we might get kicked out of our apartment again. But if I say that, I'll be taken away for sure.

"Don't worry," Aunt Mindy says. "She won't be skipping any more classes; you can count on that." She puts on her butt-kissing voice. "I've told Stevie how important high school is, how if she doesn't do her best she'll regret it for the rest of her life."

I peek through my fingers and see Mrs. Watkins hold out a chubby hand to shut Aunt Mindy up. I'm actually starting to like her.

"Let's think, here," she says. "Fortunately we caught this before Stevie racked up enough unexcused absences to land her in truancy court."

I take my hands away from my face and glare at her.

"And we're also fortunate that the Seattle School Board gives us some leeway to tailor attendance interventions to specific students." She glances at me and then back at Aunt Mindy. "So here's what I'm thinking: Given the personal stress Stevie's under, and given the fact that there are only seven days left in the school year, counting today, I'm sure our principal would be willing to waive her requirement to attend classes the final week of school."

Yes!

Aunt Mindy frowns. "I hate to disagree, but—"

"Let me finish." Mrs. Watkins gives her the that's-enough-out-of-you look she usually saves for students. "Final grades are already in. I pulled Stevie's up on the computer this morning. The good news is, she passed."

Double yes!

"The bad news is, not by much. She's not eligible for summer school, but I'd highly recommend hiring a private tutor for her over the summer."

Crap.

"If you can afford it, that is. That way she'd be in a strong position to start her sophomore year in the fall."

Of course Aunt Mindy's all over the tutor idea. Anything to make my life miserable.

Mrs. Watkins turns to me. "How does that sound?"

"Fabulous," I mutter.

She hoists herself from the desk. Her thighs jiggle into position. "I'm glad we're all on the same page," she says, and shakes Aunt Mindy's hand. "I'll be in touch."

I watch them congratulate each other and don't say a word, even though I feel like socking them both. Let them think this tutor idea is going to solve everything. At least it got Aunt Mindy to shut up about the stuff that cop told her. I even nod at Mrs. Watkins as we leave the office.

We're halfway down the hall when I hear a voice behind me: "Stevie!"

I turn around and there's Tonya, her reddish-brown dreadlocks sticking out from her pale face in all directions. She's got her cell phone in one hand and a can of Mountain Dew in the other, and she's working her gum so hard it makes my jaw ache to look at her.

"Where have you been?" she says. "I keep looking for you at

lunch and I called you a bunch of times but you never called me back and I tried to tell you about my party but—"

"Sorry. I gotta go. I'll call you later." I hustle for the front door, then turn and glance back. Tonya's standing there glaring at me. Feeling like the world's lamest excuse for a friend, I escape to the safety of the parking lot.

I just can't face talking to her right now. I just can't face anything. All I can think about is that call from Drake and the money Mom took from my heart-shaped box. And the time a few weeks ago she was on the phone with him and she didn't know I was listening and she made her voice real soft and she said, "Did you get it? Did you get the crystal?"

CHAPTER 5

It's 1:38 in the morning, and all I've been doing for the past hour and a half is trying to put this lousy day behind me. But sleep won't come. I know if I could just talk to Mom, everything would be okay. "What's eating you, baby?" she'd say, and she'd ask me to cuddle up and tell her all about it. I'd give anything to hear her voice, so I tiptoe into the living room to use the phone.

I grab the cordless and plop onto the couch. Before I dial, I close my eyes and go back to my favorite memory: I'm in our old place in Montana, and Mom is wrapping me in the blanket with little blue flowers on it. She leans over and kisses me. The memory seems so real I can almost feel her breath against my cheek. But when I open my eyes, I'm still sitting in Aunt Mindy's living room in the dark.

I dial our number. I let it ring, and even when the answering machine comes on, I keep the phone pressed to my ear, hoping. I can hear rain splatter against the windows and pound on the roof. I pray that if Mom isn't at the apartment, at least she's someplace safe and dry. I hang up.

I'm about to go back to bed. But the look on Tonya's face at school this morning pops into my head, and I know there's one more call I need to make. I ring her cell.

"Hey, Tonya. Stevie. Did I wake you up?"

Her voice is fuzzy. "It's, like, two a.m. What do you think?"

"Sorry about this morning."

"Yeah, what was up with that? And how come you never call me back? And how come you're never at school?"

"What are you, my mother?" I start to laugh, but the sound gets caught in my throat. I watch a fat raindrop slide down the window, leaving a slug trail behind. "I just . . . well . . . things have been a little crazy."

"Tell me about it! I had another fight with Mike. He tells me I can't have anybody over while he's out of town and I tell him, like, I'm sure I'm just going to sit around by myself like some kind of nun or something. Oh, by the way, did I tell you about the party we're having? It's—"

"Tonya." Sometimes you have to stop her before she zooms into hyperspace. "I'm not coming to your party."

Her voice goes high and singsongy. "The Professor's gonna be there."

The Professor is her brother's best friend—which is weird, because they're like total opposites. His real name is Van, but nobody besides teachers ever calls him that. I'm not much for crushing on guys, but if I was, I'd definitely go for him. He's smart, for one thing. And I don't mean ordinary smart, I mean super smart—like he's in all the advanced classes at school and talks about stuff like black holes and string theory and can pronounce words I've never even heard of.

For another thing, he's tall. Me and Mom, we're both short, and we like a guy we can look up to. I can definitely look up to the Professor. And I love the way he looks down at me over the top of his glasses, and the way his brownish-blond hair falls into his eyes.

I'm pretty sure he likes me too. The first time we met, at one of Tonya's parties, we hung out together the whole night. We kicked back on her deck and gazed up at the sky, and he told me all about light-years and how the stars we were looking at might not even exist anymore. Then he started stopping by my locker at school, asking if I needed help with my homework.

I haven't seen him since I quit showing up for school. I miss talking to him for sure, but what I really miss is the way he looks at me. He has this way of staring right into my eyes, like he's trying to see down into the center of me. But even that isn't enough to make me drag myself to Tonya's party.

"I don't care," I tell her. "I'm not going to spend an entire night watching you and Doug get drunk and act like morons."

"What's up with you, anyway? All of a sudden you're like Little Miss Just-Say-No, and all I want to do is have some fun and—"

"Tonya."

"Sorry. But I wish you'd tell me what's going on."

I hug one of Aunt Mindy's zebra-striped pillows. I promised myself a while back I'd never drink or do drugs again, but I haven't told Tonya yet. Actually, I haven't been all that straight with Tonya lately, and she is more or less my best friend. My only friend is more like it. Us Value Village shoppers have to stick together.

"Okay, I'll tell you what's going on. But promise you won't blab to anyone."

Last time I let her in on something big—that Mom got a job at the club—it wasn't long before the whole school knew about it. Still, I need someone to talk to. So I hug the pillow tighter and spill at least part of the mess: Aunt Mindy showing up and forcing me to stay with her. Getting hauled into Mrs. Watkins's office. Having to have a tutor. I even admit that I don't know where Mom is and I miss her and I think she might be with her creepy new boyfriend, Drake. But I don't tell her everything.

"I think we should try to find her," she says when I'm finished.

A sudden gust of wind flings a bucket of rain against the window.

"This guy Drake—you know where he lives, right? Why don't we just go to his place and see if your mom's there?"

33

Cool air prickles my bare arms. Even though the possibility of running into Drake is about as appealing as finding a dead rat on my pillow, the idea of seeing Mom makes my heart beat faster. And if Tonya was with me . . . well, maybe it wouldn't be so bad.

"You do know where he lives, right?"

"Yeah, south of downtown." Mom took me with her one time when she went to his house to pick something up. It's not the kind of place that would be easy to forget.

"So here's the plan: I'll get Mike to drop us off downtown tomorrow for a matinee. We'll take the bus from there."

Just the thought of setting foot near that house again makes my stomach churn, but I know I've got to do it.

"Okay, it's a plan. And Tonya?"

"Yeah?"

"Quit calling your dad 'Mike.'"

We decide to meet at one o'clock. I give her Aunt Mindy's address, and then I put the phone back, lean against the couch, and close my eyes. The rain sounds softer now. I'll be talking to Mom soon; maybe things will be okay.

I guess I doze off for a minute, because the sound of the toilet flushing startles me awake. Aunt Mindy must be up. As I hurry down the hall to the guest room, I notice her computer's on. I can't help myself: I slink into her room and peek at the screen.

"Symptoms of Methamphetamine Addiction" says the banner at the top.

I can't believe it. Now Aunt Mindy doesn't only think Mom's "involved" with crystal; she thinks she's addicted. Okay, so maybe Drake talked her into trying it once. Or even twice. But there's no way she's an addict. This is just another one of Aunt Mindy's sick attempts to screw up Mom's life.

I almost stomp away, but then I let my gaze drop to the list below the banner:

· Hyperactivity
· Sleep disturbances
· Excessive talking
· Mood swings
· Paranoia

I can't read any further. The letters on the screen turn into spindly-legged insects that creep into my brain.

"Stevie! I didn't know you were still up." Aunt Mindy is standing in the doorway in a baggy pink T-shirt and leopard-print slippers. Without makeup, her face looks naked.

I push past her and barrel toward the guest room, then slam the door and throw myself onto the bed.

"Stevie," Aunt Mindy says through the door, "you've got to trust me. Everything's going to be okay."

I squeeze my eyes tighter and try to pretend her voice is Mom's.

When I wake up the next morning, it's after eleven. Aunt Mindy's car is gone, so I wander into the kitchen in search of caffeine. There's a note waiting for me on the table. *Stevie,* it says. *At the studio, back by 11:30. Please load dishwasher and take out trash. We're meeting with tutor at noon. Love, M.*

I crumple the note and toss it in the garbage. Then I remember my plan with Tonya, and suddenly I'm as jumpy as if I'd just knocked back a triple mocha. I decide to skip the coffee and go get dressed. I'm going through my clothes, trying to figure out what to wear, when I find Alan's card in the pocket of my jeans. Things have been so crazy I'd almost forgotten about Tweety Bird, but now I picture the way she struggled in the dirt and hear her shrill cry. I squint at the address on the card: *8503 30th NW.* The bird clinic must be near that funky little coffee shop right along the 48 bus route. I'm thinking I should head over there someday and check on her. Then I remember Alan's stupid smirk and toss the card on the closet floor.

At 11:35 I hear Aunt Mindy come in. A couple of minutes later, there's a knock on my door.

"You're not wearing that!" she says when I open it.

I look down at my cutoffs and off-the-shoulder peasant blouse. "Obviously I am." I don't know what her problem is. She doesn't exactly look stunning in her leggings and baggy sweatshirt. I head out of the room.

She's right behind me. "Didn't you read my note? We're meeting with your tutor in twenty minutes. And by the way, I thought I asked you to load the dishwasher." She messes with the elastic on my blouse, trying to get the sleeves to cover my shoulders, and then railroads me into the kitchen.

I twist away from her hands. "Excuse me, but maybe I have other plans. My friend Tonya's picking me up at one."

"I'm sure we won't need more than half an hour with the tutor. Now get going on those dishes."

"Fine." I monkey with the front of the dishwasher until it opens.

"So, Richard Brown sounds like a nice guy," she says as she hands me a plate.

"Who's Richard Brown?" I'm trying to figure out where to put the thing.

"No, right there." She stares at me and then rolls her eyes. "Oh, I forgot. June doesn't believe in dishwashers." She shows me where to put the silverware. "Mr. Brown is your new tutor. Mrs. Watkins called yesterday afternoon and said he's agreed to work with you. He comes highly recommended."

"What do we have to meet him for, then?"

She grabs a box of dish detergent from under the sink. "You pour this in here. I want the three of us to get to know each other before you two start working together."

I try to imagine what this Mr. Brown guy is like. Probably some gray-haired grandpa-type who does volunteer work as an excuse to get out of the house.

"Now just close it and push that blue button. I'm going to change." She looks me up and down again. "Honestly, Stevie, I wish you'd wear something decent. You look like—"

"What?"

"Never mind."

I punch the button on the dishwasher and then slide my blouse even further off my shoulders.

Imagine my surprise when we walk into Starbucks and this handsome black dude stands up to greet us. I mean, this guy looks like a movie star. His hair's a little on the gray side, but his skin is so smooth, and his eyes slant at the corners like a cat's. He's wearing these cool rectangle-framed glasses, and a diamond stud sparkles in one ear.

I can tell Aunt Mindy notices him too. She fumbles with her sunglasses, and when he goes up to the counter to order, she raises her eyebrows at me and whispers, "You lucky dog! I wish I needed some tutoring."

I look away. There should be a law against old people flirting.

He comes back with our drinks. As he leans over me to set my white chocolate mocha on the table, I can smell his spicy cologne.

After a couple of minutes of stupid conversation about the weather and how much coffee everyone in Seattle drinks, Aunt Mindy says, "So tell us, Richard, what brought you to tutoring kids?"

"Please. Call me Rick," he says with a smile. "When I quit my job at Microsoft a few years ago," he says, trying to talk over the guy at the next table who's yakking away on his cell phone, "I was practically a millionaire."

A millionaire tutor? I fold my arms across my chest. *Yeah, right.*

He looks at me and laughs. "I know. My mama didn't believe it either. My daddy worked all his life, punching that clock until the day he died of a heart attack, and here I was, retiring at thirty-five.

"At first I really lived it up—traveled some, bought high-end furniture, collected wine. That was fun for about a year, then it started getting old. My whole life was about having a good time."

"Sounds okay to me!" I say.

Rick sips some foam off his cappuccino. "I know it sounds good, but believe it or not, having nothing but free time actually gets pretty boring."

I roll my eyes.

"Anyway, I decided I needed to do something more productive—something to help other people. I had kind of a difficult youth myself. We moved around a lot, so it was hard making friends. When I did, it was usually the wrong kind. I was lucky enough to have a mentor who turned me around before I ended up in trouble. That's why I decided to work with kids. Give something back, you know?"

Aunt Mindy's being totally embarrassing, staring at him with this weird look on her face. I can guess what's going through her head: rich hottie *and* nice guy—what a combination! I'm actually starting to think he's kind of a dweeb. I mean, why waste your time tutoring loser kids when you're a millionaire? Why not buy your-self a yacht and a mansion and a killer home-entertainment system? Still, I can see why she likes him. I bet Mom would go for him too, especially with him being rich and all.

While I slurp the last drops of my mocha, he and Aunt Mindy get down to business and work out a tutoring schedule. He's going to meet me in the conference room of the Northeast Library at one o'clock every Tuesday and Thursday. They tried to make it nine, but I talked them out of it. If I'm going to be tutored, I need my beauty sleep.

As Rick shrugs on his suede jacket, he looks me right in the eye and smiles. "It's great to meet you, Stevie. I think we're going to get along fine."

We all walk out to the parking lot together. When he slides into his black Maserati and turns up the R&B, I'm suddenly sold: If I have to have a tutor, it might as well be a handsome rich dude with a mega-sweet ride.

I've just finished wolfing down a PB and J when I hear a honk out-side. I race out the door before Aunt Mindy can bug me about my clothes again and climb into the back seat of Mr. Nyberg—a.k.a. Mike's—Explorer. Country music jangles on the radio. Tonya turns around and snaps her gum at me.

"I told Mike we might do a little shopping after the movie," she says with a wink.

"Hello, Mr. Nyberg," I say. "Thanks for picking me up."

He smiles at me in the rearview mirror. "No problem." Even though the air conditioning's on, his round face looks pink and sweaty. He's nice, but I can sort of get why Tonya's mom ran off with another guy.

"Jesus, Mike, I can't stand this crap." Tonya fiddles with the radio until she finds some rap. I watch his face in the mirror. He grimaces and uses his fingers to comb a few strands of hair over his bald spot, but he doesn't say anything. After twenty minutes of dodging through Saturday afternoon traffic, he pulls up in front of Pacific Place on Pine Street. Sunlight glints off high-rise windows, and the sidewalks swarm with shoppers.

"Have fun, you two. Call me when you're done."

"Thanks again, Mr. Nyberg," I say. We wait until his car disappears, then sprint over to First Avenue and catch a bus heading south.

The bus crawls through downtown. Grime covers the windows, but I can still make out the snow-capped peak of Mt. Rainier looming over the city like a giant scoop of vanilla ice cream. It's maybe fifteen minutes later when we finally roll past a corner market with some old guys sitting in front, smoking cigarettes. I pull the buzzer, and we get out at the next stop.

"So, I heard there's, like, a ton of crime in this neighborhood," Tonya says in a really loud voice as she follows me around the corner and down a narrow side street. "Crack dealers and stuff. On the news the other day—"

"Shut up," I hiss, and elbow her in the ribs. A couple of guys in baggy jeans and oversize jackets check us out from across the street. I stare at the rundown houses, hoping I can remember which one is Drake's. Finally I recognize his red truck. It's parked in front of a house in the middle of the block.

The place is just as trashy as I remembered it. The porch sags, and the white paint has mostly peeled off, leaving patches of gray. A rusted-out toilet with no lid squats in the middle of the front yard.

Tonya's eyes go wide. "Awesome."

We sneak to the side of the house and hide behind an overflowing garbage can. Tonya holds her nose and makes a gagging sound, but I hardly notice the smell. Through an opening in the curtains, in the window right across from where we're hiding, I can make out someone pacing.

"That's her!" Tonya whispers.

I tiptoe from behind the garbage can and crouch under the window, then raise myself so my eyes are just above the ledge. It's Mom all right. She's wearing her usual tight jeans and low-cut tank, and her dark curls tumble over her shoulders. But she looks thinner than I remembered, and dark circles sag under her eyes. Without her little pot belly she looks even younger, and I can see why people sometimes think we're sisters.

"Stevie!" Tonya says.

I glance back at her. She points to the window and makes a knocking motion with her hand.

I shake my head. Drake's truck is here, so chances are he is too. I turn back to the window and watch Mom move toward the sink, pick up a glass from the counter, and then continue pacing.

"Stevie!"

I look over my shoulder at Tonya again.

"Do something," she mouths.

I turn back to the window, and I'm trying to decide if I should get Mom's attention somehow, when a Buick blaring a bass beat that shakes the street pulls up in front of the house. I dive behind the garbage can and watch the car door open.

A pumped-up guy in a wifebeater and sweats, with a silver hoop in his nose and tattoos up and down both arms, swaggers up the lopsided steps and knocks at the door. Mom hurries to answer it, and he disappears inside the house. Then I see two heads, his and Mom's, show up near the side window. I sneak back under the ledge.

"Stevie! Get back here!" Tonya says. But instead I raise myself up and peek over the ledge again.

The guy reaches into the waistband of his sweats and pulls out a wad of bills. He hands them to Mom. She swipes at her nose, and her hand shakes as she counts out the money. Then she opens a drawer and passes him a little plastic bag. I can barely make out the chunks of milky rock inside.

The guy struts back to his car and peels away from the curb, trailed by the *boom, boom* of the bass. I'm still tucked under the window, wishing I could reach out and touch Mom's bare arm.

Then someone else appears. Drake. I've only seen him a couple of times, but I'd know him anywhere. He looks like he just got out of the army: military haircut, biceps bulging under the sleeves of his glaring white T-shirt. But it's his smile I see in my nightmares, tortoise lips stretched over crooked yellow teeth.

Mom hands him the bills. He stuffs them in his pocket and runs his hand across his buzzcut.

Then she starts talking to him and stroking his arm. Even from where I am, I can see the hungry look in her eyes. When he reaches into his pocket and goes to the rickety kitchen table, she follows him like a starving puppy.

A mirror, a razorblade, two lines of white powder. He sucks one up his nose with a straw, then hands the mirror to her.

I'm trembling as I lower myself from the window. I tell myself it's not what I think, that Mom would never do that.

But I know. I know in the deepest part of me, the part that hasn't learned yet how to lie.

CHAPTER 6

After dinner, which I can barely choke down, Aunt Mindy says she has something she needs to talk to me about. The last thing I'm in the mood for is one of her hissy fits, but of course she gets her way.

We sit in the living room. I'm scrunched into one corner of the couch, and Aunt Mindy perches on the love seat next to me with some papers in her lap. The lemony odor of furniture polish hangs in the air. I trace the stripes on the zebra pillow, wondering what she's going to jump down my throat about this time.

"I guess you know I've been doing some research on crystal meth," she starts out, tucking a dark curl behind her ear, "so we might as well talk about it."

I keep my eyes on the pillow.

"I'm sure you know it's a very addictive drug; doesn't take much at all to get hooked."

I scowl at her. "You hear a rumor about where Mom works, and now you think she's addicted? That's lame."

"Granted, we don't know for sure she's using crystal. But if she is . . ." She shakes her head. "I know your mom, Stevie. She's got what you'd call an addictive personality. Food, cigarettes, men . . . she never knows when to stop."

"Shows what you know. She quit smoking six months ago."

Blood rushes to her face. "I thought I saw . . . Never mind. Like you said, we don't have enough information yet, but I think some of the signs are there. Just the fact that she'd go off and leave you for almost a week—that's not normal behavior."

I open my mouth to argue, then shut it again.

Aunt Mindy holds up the papers, which I can see she printed off the Internet. "I've also been doing some research on meth rehab clinics, just in case. Apparently one of the best programs in the country is in Oregon, right near where your uncle Rob lives. I talked to him about it this afternoon—"

"You told Uncle Rob?"

"It's expensive, but between the two of us, we could pull it off, if it comes to that. We both want what's best for June."

I throw down the pillow. "You're insane! And how would you get her to go? Tie her up and drag her there?"

"Of course not." She takes a deep breath. "We'd do an intervention."

We learned in Health Ed an intervention is when you get in an addict's face and force them to admit they're screwed up. Mom would just love that. "Good luck. You don't even know where she is."

I get up to leave, but she grabs my hand. "I need your help, Stevie. You've got to tell me anything you know. Anything. Any odd behavior you remember, anyone new she's been seeing."

The awful picture flashes through my mind: Mom in the window of Drake's house. But I've already decided it wasn't really Mom. Not like an alien took over her body or something. But like the Mom in the window isn't the Mom I snuggle up with to watch wrestling when she has a Friday night off. She's not the Mom who strokes my hair while I tell her whatever's bugging me, and she's definitely not the Mom who's going to make our lives better in the not-too-distant future.

"Please," Aunt Mindy says. "This might be our only chance to help her."

I let myself imagine, just for a minute, that Mom could really go to that place and come back okay. But then I think about who she is. She lives in rundown places and drives beat-up cars partly because she has to, but mostly to show people she doesn't give a crap. She can't keep a job because she hates being bored, and she gets into trouble because she can't stand anyone telling her how to live. "Honey pie," she always tells me, "we're free spirits. You and me, we live by our own rules." That's what I love about her.

"Stevie?" Aunt Mindy says. "Will you help me?"

I look her right in the eyes and make my voice tight, sharp, and cold.

"No."

I stumble into the guest room and slide under the covers. All I want to do is go to sleep, but my mind is on overdrive. When I finally do doze off, I have these bizarre dreams: Rick making out with Mom in the back seat of his Maserati. Aunt Mindy crushing Tweety Bird's head with the heel of her shoe. I even start to have the one about Mom wrapping me in the blanket. She leans over and kisses me, and then she whispers in my ear, "I'll take care of you." I jolt awake and remember what happened at Drake's. And I don't feel taken care of at all.

I spend all day Sunday avoiding Aunt Mindy. Tonya calls me on my new cell and says I should come over, but I tell her I'm busy. When she asks me what the deal was yesterday, I tell her Mom and Drake started making out, and I wasn't about to talk to Mom with that jerk around. I couldn't tell her what I really saw. No one in the world, not even Tonya, would understand.

But when Monday morning comes, I decide I can't stand to spend another day hanging out in the guest room. As soon as I'm sure Aunt Mindy's gone, I jump out of bed, throw on some clothes, and, ignoring her stupid list of chores, race out to the bus stop. The old neighborhood is calling me.

It's one of those mornings that cons you into thinking it's already summer, where the Olympic Mountains look like gray and white cutouts against a perfect blue sky. If there's one thing I love about Seattle, it's the mountains. The two ranges line up on either side like they're guarding the city, the Cascades to the east and the Olympics in the west. But my favorite is Mt. Rainier, which towers in the south like a bouncer at the front door, daring anyone to get by.

I sit on the nearly empty bus and close my eyes, pretending I'm up there, hanging out by some alpine lake. But the haven't-had-a-shower-in-two-weeks stink from the old man two rows behind me kind of spoils the illusion.

The bus barrels down 85th, past the street that winds behind the cemetery. The street where I found Tweety Bird. Once again I picture her, so lost and helpless, and I decide seeing her again, making sure she's okay, would be worth the risk of running into Alan. As soon as I spot the little coffee shop up ahead, I ring the buzzer. The driver lets me off on 30th Northwest, and I head north, searching for anything that looks like a bird hospital. It's an ordinary neighborhood with houses and driveways and kids playing in front yards—not the kind of place you'd expect to find a clinic.

Then I see the sign. It's on a wooden post in front of a boxy gray house that looks like all the others on the street. *On the Wing* it says, and in smaller letters just below, *Bird Rehabilitation Center*. Before I can change my mind, I march to the front door and ring the bell.

A gray-haired woman in black pants and a pink cotton blouse answers. A pair of glasses hangs on a chain around her neck. She looks like somebody's grandma, and I find myself wishing I hadn't worn my black midriff top with the two white buttons right over my nipples.

"Can I help you, dear?" she asks.

I cross my arms over my chest. "I found this baby bird . . ."

She cranes her neck to look behind me. "Do you have it with you?"

"No, I mean I found it the other day. By the cemetery. This guy Alan talked me into letting him bring it here."

"Oh, are you the one who found that wonderful little robin?" She opens the screen door wide. "Well, come in, come in. I'm Valerie, by the way. You'll be happy to know the robin's doing just fine."

She leads me through an ordinary-looking living room and kitchen to a room at the back of the house with at least twenty cages and laundry baskets stacked against the walls. The air is filled with squawks, chirps, and the rustle of wings. I look around for Alan, but there's no sign of him.

"Alan works here, right?"

"Yes. He lives here too, but he took my car out for supplies. He should be back in a little while, if you want to wait."

Alan lives here? I wrinkle my nose, and not only because the room smells kind of like a pet store. "That's okay."

She leads me to a row of incubators against the back wall. "There it is, contented as can be."

I peer inside the incubator. It's Tweety Bird all right, huddled in that little berry-basket nest. Aside from having a few more feathers, she looks pretty much the same as when I found her.

"Would you like to try feeding it?"

I remember learning that mother robins eat worms and puke them into their babies' mouths. "Uh, no, thanks."

But she holds out a pair of latex gloves. "Put these on. You'll do fine." Then she hands me a syringe filled with some gross brown stuff.

"I thought robins ate worms."

"We'll get to those. But this formula is as close as we can get to what the mother bird regurgitates for her young."

I stare at the syringe. Artificial bird puke. Nice.

She slides open the door of the incubator, and Tweety Bird starts chirping like crazy. She opens her beak so wide I can see straight into her bright yellow throat.

"It's okay, honey pie," I coo at the little bird. "I've got your food right here."

Valerie puts a finger to her lips. "We don't talk to them while we feed them. And you'll want to avoid eye contact."

That makes no sense to me. I mean, if you're going to go to all the trouble of taking care of a bird, why can't you make friends with it? But since I'm standing with a goop-filled syringe in my hand and Tweety Bird is opening her beak wide enough to swallow it whole, I decide I should probably feed now and ask questions later.

"What the bird's doing is called 'gaping,' and it means it's ready for food. So you're going to take the syringe . . ." She holds my wrist and guides my hand toward Tweety Bird's open beak. ". . . And stick it in as far as you can. No, farther than that."

I pull my hand back. "But she'll choke!"

"She? There's as much chance this bird is a male—we wouldn't be able to tell until a year from now, when its feathers change color. If it's a female, those spots will disappear, and its breast will turn a pale red-orange." She takes hold of my wrist again. She has bony old-lady fingers. "It won't choke if you get that syringe way down in there, past its glottis—which is that little opening."

This time I manage to get the syringe in far enough. I close my eyes and squirt about half the contents down Tweety Bird's throat.

"See? That wasn't so bad. Look, it's ready for more."

I open my eyes and there's Tweety Bird, chirping and gaping again. It takes a few more syringe-fulls before she—I just know she's a girl—finally settles down. When I think I'm done, Valerie hands me a pair of tweezers and a dish full of wiggling worms.

"Let's see if it'll eat a couple of these. Pick them up by the tail if you can—that way they're easier for the bird to swallow."

I seriously can't believe I'm doing this, but I poke around in the dish with the tweezers until I manage to grab one of the worms by the tail. Then I drop it into Tweety Bird's waiting beak. "Oh, gross," I say.

"You're a natural," Valerie says. "Would you like to feed a few more? I could use the help."

Part of me wants to get away before Alan shows up, but for some reason it's hard to leave. In the next half hour I feed a baby crow, two more robins, a sparrow, and a finch. With each feeding I'm less nervous about sticking in the syringe, more confident about picking up worms and berries with the tweezers.

I try to picture Alan feeding a baby bird. "Alan does this too?"

Valerie smiles. "Oh, yes. He's wonderful with the birds. And they're wonderful for him."

I'm about to ask what she means when I see a cage covered with a black cloth.

"What's in there?"

"A jay that a woman brought in early this morning. The poor thing's stunned."

"What happened to it?"

"Flew into a window, probably. It happens a lot. The bird's sailing along, thinking it's free and clear, and then . . . *boom!* It slams into a wall of glass."

Once when I was a kid, back in Montana, we were driving along the road and a bird flew right into Mom's windshield. It made a sickening *whump,* and I begged her to stop the car so I could see if it was still alive. It lay there by the side of the road, and it wasn't until I got closer that I could see it was still breathing.

"It's gone," Mom had said, waving her hand. "Leave it."

I look up at Valerie. "Can you do anything for it?"

"It probably has a concussion, so all I can do is keep it quiet for a couple of hours, so the blood has a chance to drain away from its brain. But there's no guarantee that it will live. When one of God's creatures is hurting, it's our duty to do our best to help it heal, but ultimately it's in His hands."

I've never been big on the God stuff, but her words press against a sore place inside me. I should have at least moved that bird off the road, but I knew Mom wouldn't let me touch it. I always hated the thought that I left it lying there when maybe, just maybe, it had a chance to fly again.

I'm about to ask her more about the bird when Alan bursts into the room with a plastic grocery bag in each hand.

"Sorry it took me so long," he says. "I had to stop for gas." Then he catches sight of me, and his mouth twists into its usual smirk. "Well, well. Look who's here."

"Yes," says Valerie, "I've been having a delightful time with your friend. Goodness, I never got your name, dear."

"Stevie."

"What an unusual name. Is that short for something?"

I glance at Alan, who's pretending to unpack the grocery bags. But I can tell he's waiting for me to say something stupid. "My mom named me after her favorite singer, Stevie Nicks."

"Oh, yes, I remember her. Fleetwood Mac, right? She sang that one song, something about 'tell me sweet little lies.'"

I look at her in surprise. I'd figured her for more of the Easy Listening type. "Yeah. My mom loves to dance to that one."

Alan starts doing a lame imitation of a stripper, gyrating his hips and undoing the top buttons of his army jacket. "I'll bet she does."

"Shut up! She's not a stripper, she's a dancer."

"Yeah, right."

"Alan!" For the first time Valerie's voice is sharp. "Please go clean the aviaries."

He shoots me a dirty look, then takes his time leaving the room.

Valerie watches him go. Then she shakes her head and turns back to me. "Don't mind Alan. He didn't mean anything by it." She puts her hand on my arm. "You love your mother, don't you?"

I pull away. "Why wouldn't I?"

She gives me a long look and then says, "How would you like to come back and help me with the birds a couple of times a week? Maybe Mondays and Wednesdays? I can't pay you, but—"

"Yes," I say before she can finish.

On the bus ride home, my mind keeps drifting back to that bird that hit our windshield in Montana, and I keep hearing Valerie's words: "When one of God's creatures is hurting, it's our duty to help it heal."

Aunt Mindy's in her bedroom. I knock on the door. "I think we need to help my mom," I say.

She sits me down on the couch, and I tell her what I saw at Drake's. Not everything, but enough to make her say, "What's his name, Stevie?"

"His name's Drake," I tell her. "Drake Uttley."

CHAPTER 7

Aunt Mindy promised we'd talk about Mom the next morning, but she forgot that Mrs. Watkins had set up a home interview with a social worker from CPS. The lady shows up early and asks a bunch of questions. She wants to know how long Mom's been working at the club, how often she left me alone, stuff like that. Of course Aunt Mindy didn't tell me she was coming, so I didn't have time to think up any good answers. I figure things can't get much worse than they already are, so I mostly tell the truth. She gives me her card "in case anything comes up." Whatever that's supposed to mean. Then Aunt Mindy takes off for work before I can ask her if she's planning to track Mom down at Drake's today.

On top of that, it's Tuesday, the day of my first tutoring session with Rick. I decide to celebrate (ha, ha) by dressing up a little, so I wiggle into a retro black cocktail dress and slip on a pair of gold strappy sandals I found at the bottom of the Goodwill discount barrel. I check myself out in the mirror. Mom would be proud.

I'm due to meet Rick in the library conference room at one. By twelve-thirty I'm standing at the door to the room, feeling so antsy I'd chain smoke if I could stand the taste of cigarettes.

He shows up at 1:03 with an armload of books and breezes past me. "Hey, Stevie. Nice threads." He plops the books on one of the round tables and pulls out an orange plastic chair. "You ready to get to work?"

I take a seat beside him. While he's shuffling through his notes,

I scoot a little closer so I can smell his cologne and study his diamond stud.

"Let's start with math," he says.

Wouldn't you know he'd pick my absolute worst subject?

"I got this book from your school counselor. Do you remember where you were when you started having trouble?"

He flips through the pages. Algorithms. Equations. N equals X plus 3. I don't remember any of it. I must look as sick as I feel, because he says, "We'll just start at the beginning, then."

He opens to page one and jots the first problem on a piece of lined paper, then slides it over to me. I take the pencil he gives me and stare at the problem as hard as I can, but nothing happens. It's like everything I ever learned about math has flown out of my brain. I stare and stare and chew on the end of the pencil.

Finally I push the paper away. "What do I need to know this stuff for, anyway? It's not like I'm going to be a physicist or something."

Rick gives me a gentle smile that crinkles the corners of his cat eyes. "What *are* you planning to be, Stevie?"

Oh, God. There it is: The Question. When they asked us in kindergarten what we wanted to be when we grew up, it was easy. A policewoman. A movie star. An astronaut. But now I know you don't get to be one of those things when you can barely make it through school and your mom can't even pay rent on the cruddiest apartment in Ballard. Mrs. Watkins is always bugging me about The Future and am I going to take the SAT and apply to college. But how can I think about that when I don't even know where I'll be living next week?

"No clue," I admit.

"There must be something you care about, something that makes you really happy."

What makes me happy? When Drake doesn't call for three days straight. When we don't have to pick up and move one more time.

Rick takes one look at me and says, "Tell you what: Let's move on to a different subject."

Gladly.

We switch to Biology, which seems completely pointless, and then U.S. Government, which is the world's biggest snoozefest. To save myself from death by boredom, I imagine Rick and Mom together. I see them getting married and him buying us a humungous house and taking us for rides in his Maserati. I'm just starting to plan our trip to Hawaii when he raps his knuckles gently against my head.

"Hello. Anybody in there?"

Turns out I was in outer space when he gave me my assignment for Thursday, which is to write a review of a book I've read recently. I tell him I can't even remember the last time I cracked one open.

"Perfect," he says. "Now is a great time to start. Your homework is to find a book that interests you and read it."

Homework? I can't believe it. Here it is, almost the start of summer vacation, and I'm stuck in a library doing homework.

He stacks the textbooks into a neat pile. "I'm going to let you hang on to these. No pressure or anything—open them up and flip through them if you feel like it. Just to get back into practice."

If he wasn't so danged nice, I'd give him my "whatever" look, but instead I dredge up a smile. "Sure."

After Rick leaves, I consider hanging out in the library to look for a book, but the thought of staring at all those titles makes me tired.

So I lug the textbooks back to Aunt Mindy's and shove them under the guest room bed. Then I slide out of the dress and pull on a pair of sweats. The afternoon sun is streaming through the window, so I lower the blinds.

To take my mind off Rick's questions about The Future, I close my eyes and go to our NTD House. This time I make it a funky little place out in the country. It's got furniture made of logs and sticks, and there's a real tree growing in the living room. I laugh but get so into it that I grab a piece of paper and a pencil and start to draw.

I'm just putting the finishing touches on the second bathroom, which has a shower that looks like a waterfall, with water tumbling over rocks, when there's a knock on the guest room door. "Stevie?" says Aunt Mindy. "Can I come in?"

I look at the clock; I can't believe it's after five.

"Hang on," I tell her. I fold up the NTD House drawings and stick them between the pages of the math book. "What do you want?"

Worry lines crease her forehead. "Can I sit down?"

I scoot over and make a spot for her on the bed. The way she's picking at the maroon polish on her thumbnail makes me nervous.

"It's about the intervention. Things are moving a little faster than I expected."

My throat goes dry. I swallow hard.

"I got on the phone with Uncle Rob this morning, and we lined up an intervention specialist. I gave him the name of that Drake fellow, and we were planning to try to track your mom down at his place this weekend. But she beat us to it. She called me at work to-day and asked to borrow some money."

Of course: It's almost the first. The day our rent is due.

"I said I'd meet her at the apartment tonight at eight. She doesn't know that Uncle Rob and Dave, the intervention specialist, will be there too."

Typical Aunt Mindy move, getting everybody to gang up on Mom when she's least expecting it. I hug my legs to my chest and frown. "You lied to her."

"Now, sweetie, don't look at me like that. I'm only trying to do what's best for your mom."

"And you think what's best is playing a dirty trick on her?"

She reaches out to put her hand on my shoulder, but I jerk away.

"I'm sorry you're upset. But Dave thinks we need to take advantage of this opportunity, and he's had a lot of experience with these things. Anyway, I didn't come to ask your permission. I came to ask if you want to be there."

My jaw drops a mile. For sure I want Mom to get some help, but I'd be nuts to let Aunt Mindy drag me into this lame setup. "No way."

"You could make a big difference, Stevie."

I can't see how. Mom always does whatever she wants. And how could I look her in the eye when I'm the one who ratted her out in the first place?

"I'm not going," I tell her, and turn away.

I spend the next couple of hours staring at the ceiling. At first I worry that not showing up at the intervention will be a big mistake. I picture Mom framed in the window of Drake's house with the skin of her cheeks stretched tight and those dark circles underneath her eyes.

Then a sharp claw of anger rips at my gut. If Aunt Mindy had kept her big nose out of our lives, none of this would be happening. Let her do the dirty work.

At seven-thirty Aunt Mindy pokes her head in and says, "Wish me luck." I feel cold and hollow, like someone scooped my insides out, and I wonder if I should have kept my mouth shut about the whole thing. There's no way I can sit here all night, thinking about what's going on at the apartment. As soon as I hear her car pull away, I try out my new cell.

"Hey, Tonya. That party still happening? Because I think I might be up for it after all."

By the time the bus gets me to Tonya's, the party's hopping. Lights blaze in every window, and people are spilling onto the front porch. I jostle my way through the maze of sweaty bodies. Everyone's shouting to be heard over the rap music on the living room sound system; they've got it turned up so loud every beat feels like a minor earthquake. The whole place reeks of beer. Even if it is the last week of school, only Tonya and Doug could get this many kids together on a Tuesday night.

"Stevie!" Tonya's waving a bottle at me from across the room. Her hair is a mass of ribbons, a different color tied to each dreadlock.

I surf through the crowd till I'm standing beside her.

"Isn't this awesome?" she says. "Like, everybody's here. All of Doug's friends, and guess what?" She leans in close, and I can smell the alcohol on her breath. "The Professor said he'd show."

I'm glad I took the time to change into my red vinyl skirt, leopard print top, and white go-go boots. The pair of dangly bead earrings Mom made really pulls my look together.

I grab the bottle of rum from her. "Give me that thing."

I take a big swallow, and for a moment, my throat feels like it's on fire. Then a warm feeling spreads across my chest. I take a second one. I forgot how much better this makes you feel, how it puts you somewhere outside yourself.

"Go, Stevie!" Tonya says and claps me on the back as I take a third swallow and then a fourth. She shouts something about mixed drinks and disappears toward the kitchen. I wedge my way back into the crowd. Someone hands me a beer, and before long I'm dancing and laughing and doing a fine imitation of a party animal, if I do say so myself. I keep looking around for the Professor, hoping he's catching my act, but I don't see him anywhere.

An hour or so later I'm standing by the speakers, swaying to the tunes and nursing a beer, when I feel a hand on my shoulder.

"Hey, beautiful."

I open my eyes and there's this guy I recognize from school. Cole, I think his name is. He's one of those blond jock types, the kind that doesn't usually give me the time of day. But right now his watery blue eyes are staring into mine.

He takes the plastic cup from my hand and sets it on one of the speakers. "Let's dance."

Before I can say anything, he pulls me into the sea of gyrating bodies. There's not much room to move, so we just kind of stand there, inches apart, grooving to the beat.

He brings his mouth close to my ear. "I like the way you dance."

I smile at him. I kind of like the way I'm dancing too. The music fills me, swiveling my shoulders and hips. I can almost imagine I'm Mom.

His gaze slides up and down my body. "Sweet."

It feels good to have him look at me this way, like I'm something special. And I don't mind that some of the girls from school, the ones who whisper about me behind my back, are seeing him look at me too.

The song ends, and a slow one comes on. Everyone around us couples up.

"Well, thanks," I say, and step away.

He grabs my hand. "Uh-uh. You're not getting off that easy."

He pulls me in close. With my face buried in his chest, I can feel the steady thump of his heart. I wonder what the Professor would think if he saw me dancing like this. But the Professor's not here, and I like the sensation of Cole's arms around me, so I decide to go with it.

As we shuffle side to side, his hand moves along my back, sliding toward the gap between the bottom of my top and the waistband of my skirt. When his fingers touch skin, I draw in a sharp breath.

"Let's go outside," he whispers.

We wander into the backyard, where a bunch of guys are hanging out by the keg, downing tequila shooters.

"How about one for the lady?" Cole says.

The guys hoot and holler when I slam down three of them. Cole tries to hand me another beer.

"I've had enough."

"Go ahead." He slings his arm tight across my shoulders. "I've got you covered."

I feel safe and warm tucked close to him, so I take the beer. But the cup has a hard time finding my mouth.

He uses his finger to dab away the liquid that dribbles down my chin. "How about a little kiss?"

He doesn't wait for me to answer, just smashes his lips against mine. Then he slips his tequila-soaked tongue in my mouth and starts swishing it around. His breath is hot and noisy.

The guys form a circle around us. "Get in there, Cole!" one of them yells. They all laugh and cheer.

I'm not feeling special anymore. In fact, I'm feeling dirty. I try to pull away, but my legs are rubbery and he's holding me so tight.

With his mouth still squashed against mine, he grabs my butt with one hand and slides his other hand under the front of my top. The mob of crazy-drunk guys presses in so close, I swear I can hear them slobber. I feel like a trapped animal. I try to twist out of his grasp, but his hold tightens even more, and he works his hand up under my bra.

Just when I'm scared things are going to get even uglier, someone moves up behind Cole and grabs his shoulder.

"You want to let her go?" says a low, calm voice, and I know it's the Professor. He yanks Cole off me.

"Hey, what's your problem?" Cole says. "I'm just giving her what she wants."

I try to argue, but nothing comes out of my mouth. My whole body is shaking.

The Professor gives Cole a shove. "Grow up, loser." Then he puts his arm around my waist and leads me toward the house. The crowd of guys parts to let us through.

"You okay?" he asks me.

I nod and readjust my bra.

"Let's get out of here. I'll drive you home."

"Gotta say bye to Tonya."

We stumble back into the house. It's gotten even more crowded, and we have to weave our way through throngs of kids, most of them wasted out of their minds. We run into Doug in the hallway. I'd wondered where he'd been hiding—he usually hangs out by the keg.

"Hey, Prof," he says, "How's it goin'?" He looks at us through bloodshot eyes, but he doesn't sound drunk. He nudges the Professor. "Come back to my room for a minute, if you get a chance. I got something to show you."

"Go ahead," I say as I spot Tonya.

The Professor smiles down at me. "I'll meet you out front in ten minutes."

Tonya's in the kitchen with Laura Rogers, this girl from school. They're standing at the table, stuffing their faces with chips and onion dip. From behind they look hilarious, with Laura's sleek blond hair next to Tonya's crazy dreads. Tonya thinks Laura is cool because she spent a few days in juvie. I think she's an idiot. I move in closer, trying to stay clear of the smoke that drifts from Laura's cigarette.

"And it was in, like, the creepiest part of town," Tonya's saying. "I mean, there was a friggin' toilet in the front yard. So we hid behind this garbage can and—"

Laura nudges her and points her thumb toward me.

Tonya swivels. Her face goes bright red. "Stevie! I thought you were out back."

I just stare at her, partly because I'm mad and partly because the room is spinning.

She puts her hand on my arm and steers me away from Laura. "I'm sorry, okay? I know I said I wouldn't—"

"I'm leaving." I'm pissed at Tonya—and myself. I was an idiot to think coming here would help me forget about Mom. It's like she's following me everywhere.

"Don't leave. Hey, it's only two-thirty. We're getting another keg, and this party's about to start rocking."

I pull away from her. "Going home."

◆

And then I'm in the passenger seat of the Professor's Subaru, smelling his pine-scented air freshener and staring at the stale corn nuts on the floor. It takes forever to get back to Aunt Mindy's, because I keep forgetting where he's supposed to turn. He finally stops in front of the house. He kills the engine and opens his window.

The cool air's sobering me up a little. At least enough to notice that he seems nervous. He's usually so laid back, but tonight he keeps scratching at his cheek and jiggling his left leg.

"Thanks for getting me out of there," I say.

He pushes his glasses up the bridge of his nose. "Hey, just wish I'd shown up sooner."

I'm not about to tell him, but I'm actually glad he didn't show up any earlier. I'm glad he didn't see me dancing with Cole. We sit for a minute without saying anything. I hug my bare arms.

"You cold?" He shuts the window and slides his arm across the back of my seat. He must be more nervous than ever, because his leg's jiggling a million miles an hour.

I glance at him. "I hope you don't think . . . I know he said I wanted to, but I—"

"Don't even go there," he says, waving his hand. "Cole's a moron." He smiles at me. "Plus I know you're not like that."

He starts to play with my hair, twirling it around his finger. He puts his hand on my cheek and turns me to face him. I'm kind of hoping he'll kiss me. But instead he says, "You need to watch out, Stevie. There are plenty of guys like Cole looking for a chance to hit on you. They think just because your mom, well . . . you know."

I know. As soon as Tonya spilled the news about where Mom works, guys started following me in the halls and saying stuff like will I give them a lap dance and when's my next show.

"And I'd stay away from booze if I were you. Messes up your judgment and slows your reaction time."

Now he's starting to sound like my big brother, but I don't mind.

I snuggle in closer. "What are you, the Party Police?"

"Naw, nothing like that." He laughs and gives my shoulder a squeeze. "I don't want to see you getting hurt."

I turn toward him, and he looks deep into my eyes. His pupils are huge and dark behind his glasses. He moves toward me, and now I'm sure we're going to kiss. I shut my eyes.

Just as our lips come together, there's a loud rap on the passenger-side window. We jump apart. I look out to see Aunt Mindy standing next to the car in her robe and slippers. She knocks again and motions me out with a jerk of her head.

"Gotta go," I tell him.

"Right."

I stumble out of the car, practically knocking Aunt Mindy over. The cool air slaps my cheeks. I have to lean against her as she steers me into the house.

"Oh, honestly, Stevie."

"Leave me alone." I stagger into the guest room and fling myself onto the bed. I know I should ask her how the intervention went, but I'm too wasted to talk. Even with my eyes closed, the room spins, and images of the evening replay in my mind.

Then, as I slide toward sleep, my thoughts turn to Mom. We've had some good times together, for sure. Hitting the thrift stores on Saturday afternoons, chowing down on burgers and fries at the McDonald's across the street, making fun of all the Barbie wannabes ordering their salads with low-fat dressing. Dreaming about the future and living by our own rules. She's the only person in the world who totally gets me, and now she probably hates me for turning her in. Or maybe she did agree to go to rehab, and I won't see her until she gets out. Either way, it's all my fault. I curl up on my side and let my thoughts fall away.

I don't know if it's real or a dream, but sometime in the night I feel someone slip off my shoes and tuck a warm blanket under my chin. I'd give anything for it to be Mom.

I wake up the next morning and I know I must look like hell on toast. My head throbs, and my mouth feels like a horny toad crawled inside and died there. If Mom was here she'd say, "All you need is a hair of the dog," and she'd pour me a big cup of black coffee with a shot of whiskey in it. I have to pee, but instead I pull the covers over my head to block out the sun that's hammering at the window. I'd rather wet the bed than risk facing Aunt Mindy right now.

But before long, my bladder's so full I'm about to pop. I stumble into the hallway and just about crash into Aunt Mindy, who's carrying a tray with some breakfast on it. The smell of eggs sends my stomach into my throat.

"About time," she says. "I made you some—"

"Gotta puke." I dash into the bathroom and shut the door.

Afterward, I rinse my mouth in the sink with toothpaste and then sit on the toilet with my head in my hands. The smell of Aunt Mindy's papaya shower gel makes my head hurt worse.

I know I can't hang out on the toilet all day. The hallway is clear, so I'm hoping Aunt Mindy gave up and went away. But no, there she is, sitting in the white wicker rocking chair, which she's pulled up to my bed. She's got on jeans and a Pilates Body T-shirt.

She nods at the plate of eggs and a mug of coffee on the TV tray beside her. "I thought you might like to eat in here."

"Thanks." I wait for her to leave, but she doesn't, so I slip back into bed and pick up the coffee.

Okay, I think, *here it comes.* The lecture about the Dangers of

Drinking and Unprotected Sex, the you're-grounded-for-the-rest-of-your-life speech and all that. But she just asks, "How's the coffee?"

"Great." Which it is, actually. I was expecting her usual coffee-flavored dishwater, but she's made it strong.

"Look, Stevie, I don't blame you for last night. If I were your age, I'd probably have done the same thing."

Yeah, right. Like Miss Perfect would screw up the way I did. I take another sip of coffee and study her face over the rim of the mug. If there's one thing I don't trust, it's Aunt Mindy pretending she gets me.

"You should have some eggs. You need protein."

I shake my head, and not only because the sight of them makes me want to puke again. I'm stalling and I know it, and I know she knows I know it.

"Don't you want to hear how the intervention went?"

I scoot away from her and just about spill my coffee, but I don't answer.

"Well, I'm going to tell you whether you want to hear it or not. It was rough, but it worked. Your mom admitted she has a problem. She drove down to Portland with Uncle Rob last night, and he's taking her to the rehab clinic this morning."

I set down the mug. Coffee sloshes onto the eggs. "You're messing with me, right?"

"No, I'm just telling you what really happened. Dave's good at what he does. He caught her up in her own lies, and pretty soon she had no choice. She had to admit she's hooked on crystal."

I can't imagine in a million years that Mom would admit that, but I guess it must be true. I stare at the coffee mug and try to hold on while my world turns upside down.

"How long does she have to stay there?"

She purses her lips. "Ninety days, sweetheart."

For sure I want Mom to get better, but the thought of putting up with Aunt Mindy for the rest of the summer makes me want to scream.

Her voice gets all cheery. "This place has an eighty-percent recovery rate. And I think June's going to love it there. It's right by the ocean. Maybe it's because we grew up in Montana, where the only water is in lakes and rivers, but you know she's always had a thing about the ocean."

My mind is full of questions: What if the treatment doesn't work? Or what if it works too well and the Mom that comes back isn't like my old Mom at all?

Aunt Mindy's still talking. "The summer will go by before you know it," she's saying, and "Maybe when she comes back, she'll get herself a decent job." But I can barely hear her. The questions keep echoing over and over in my brain: *What if . . . ? What if . . . ? What if . . . ?*

She pushes herself from the chair and says, "One more thing, Stevie. The boy you were with last night, was he drinking too?"

I frown at her. "No."

"Well, I'm glad for that. But you know you could have called me. I'd rather get woken up in the middle of the night than have you ride home with a kid who's had too much to drink."

I knew she wouldn't let me off without a lecture. She finally leaves for work. I snuggle back under the covers and wonder what's going to happen to me now. When I moved in here a week ago, I never thought it would be for the entire summer. At least I've got the birds to keep me busy . . .

"Crap!" I yell, and jump out of bed. It's Wednesday, and I was supposed to be at On the Wing two hours ago. Trying to ignore the pounding in my head and the lurching of my stomach, I throw on a T-shirt and jeans and hop the first bus to Ballard.

It's cloudy and still, which makes me feel like the whole world's in a coma. I race the two blocks from the bus stop to On the Wing and slip in the back door, the way Valerie told me to. Alan's kneeling by one of the incubators. When he sees me, he stands and stuffs his big paws in his pockets. Today his dark hair is slicked back and held in place by his sunglasses, which sit on top of his head.

He looks me up and down. "Nice of you to finally show up."

"Give me a break. I had a rough morning, okay?"

"Aww, that's too bad. Too much partying last night?"

"Where's Valerie?"

"She waited around for you. She just left for the dentist."

"Oh." I cross my arms over my chest.

"So, are you just going to stand there," he says, "or are you going to get some work done?"

I wish I could leave, but I made a promise to Valerie. I go straight to Tweety Bird's incubator. She's huddled in her little nest, but when I get close, she stretches her neck and gapes. Even though I know it's all about the food, it still feels good that she's glad to see me.

"Want me to start feeding?" I ask.

"We're out of formula. Did Valerie show you how to make it yet?"

"No."

"Then watch and learn."

His I'm-a-bird-expert attitude is driving me nuts, but I am curious what fake bird barf is made of. He plugs in the blender, then takes a bowl of mushy brown stuff out of the fridge. It smells like old dog food. The coffee I drank earlier does a three-sixty in my stomach.

"Eeww. What is that?"

"Ferret chow. It's high in protein, and it's got similar carbs to what birds feed their babies in the wild. We soak it in water overnight to make it soft enough to feed through the syringes." He scoops up a spoonful and shoves it in my face. "Want some?"

I stumble backward. "Gross!"

He grins and comes toward me with the spoon. "Yum, yum."

"Cut it out." I'm trying to look mad, but I can't hold back a nervous giggle.

"Open up. Time for breakfast."

I shriek and duck away from him.

"Okay, then, I'll eat it myself." He throws his head back, opens his mouth wide, and dangles the spoon above it.

"Oh. Gross. Don't," I say, half gasping, half laughing.

He brings the spoon closer and closer to his mouth, then at the last minute pulls it away.

A big smile spreads across his face—not his usual mean smirk, but a real smile that shows the gap between his front teeth and lights up his eyes, which I'm glad for once aren't hiding behind those sunglasses.

"Had you going there," he says.

I roll my eyes. "You're a freak."

He goes back to his usual grouchy self, but things aren't as tense between us. He dumps the waterlogged ferret chow into the blender, along with yogurt, dried egg whites and some disgusting yellow stuff from a jar.

"What's that?"

"Baby-chicken food," he yells over the whirring noise. Then

there's a loud *pop,* and the top of the blender shoots off. Alan flips the switch before the mush flies everywhere, but it's still a mess. A brownish-yellow puddle spreads across the counter.

He fumbles around under the sink. "Great. We're out of rags. Go grab me a towel, would you?"

"Where?"

"The bathroom closet." He nods toward the other side of the house. "Through Valerie's bedroom."

Just like I expected, her room is full of old-lady stuff: a vase of dried purple flowers by the window, a corny painting of mountains and geese on the wall above the bed. Then a framed photo on her dresser catches my eye. A dark-haired man in a suit and skinny tie smiles out at me, and next to him a boy about my age holds up a baseball glove. I move in to take a closer look. The boy has Valerie's eyes.

I hand Alan the towel. "So, you do this now instead of going to school?" I ask as he wipes up the mess and then pours the rest of the food into yogurt cups.

"It's summer."

Well, technically school doesn't get out for two days, but whatever. "You know what I mean."

"Well, then, yep."

"Isn't that against the law or something?"

"Hey, I'm seventeen. As long as I'm working, I don't have to go to school if I don't want to." He hands me one of the cups and a syringe. "I notice you haven't been exactly burning up the halls of old Ballard High, either."

"I don't want to talk about it."

"You brought it up." He smiles that real smile again. "Hey, how about this? I'll spill my story if you tell me yours."

"I don't know. Mine's kind of long."

He shrugs. "We got nothing to do but feed a bunch of birds."

Truth is, I'm dying to tell someone. Even though Alan is the last person on earth I thought I'd be telling it to, I have a feeling I'm not the only one who's had a rough ride.

So while I poke the syringe down Tweety Bird's throat, I tell him about the night Aunt Mindy showed up at the apartment. As I dangle a wiggling worm from a pair of tweezers, I tell him about having to stay with her and get tutored by Rick. While I refill a food dish for a couple of noisy crows, I tell him what I saw at Drake's, and last of all, as I use a mister to wet down some swallows, I tell him about Mom going into rehab. I keep expecting him to chime in with some nasty comment, but he doesn't say a word.

Finally I'm finished. We stare at each other across the room. Then, with a totally straight face, he says, "Sounds like your life just let a bunch of bad farts."

I open my mouth to give him a hard time, but instead I burst out laughing. "Bad farts, that's good," I say. He laughs too.

We continue feeding, but every few minutes one of us snorts. I'm actually starting to feel glad Valerie isn't around. But when I get to an injured jay, I stop laughing.

"Hey," I say, "I can't get this jay to gape."

"Yeah, that's a tricky one." He comes up next to me and peers into the cage. He's so close that his shoulder touches mine, but this time I don't pull away. He holds one hand over the jay's head and moves his fingers toward his thumb and then away, like a beak opening and closing.

"What are you doing?"

"Sometimes a bird will gape for me when I do this. It thinks my hand is its mother's beak."

Sure enough, the jay opens its mouth wide, and I manage to squirt in a syringe-full of food.

"That doesn't seem fair. I mean, obviously you're not its mother."

He looks at me like I'm crazy. "So? The bird got what it needed, didn't it?"

"It just seems like you're tricking it."

"Hey, if we weren't willing to con them a little, half these birds would be dead right now."

I look around at the cages and incubators. I don't know if you can tell how a bird feels, but I could swear these birds look happy. Or contented, at least, as Valerie would say. They don't seem to remember they ever had mothers.

As I watch Alan hunched over the jay, opening and closing his big hand some more, I decide maybe I was wrong about him. This Alan seems really different from the guy who treats people like dirt, the one everyone was scared of at school.

"Okay, it's your turn," I say as I stick the syringe down the jay's throat a second time. "How come you're not in school?"

"Wouldn't you like to know."

"Wait a second. I just told you my entire life story."

He turns to me and the old smirk is back. "I guess you're pretty stupid, then."

"But you said—"

"I say a lot of things." His eyes are so cold and hard, he might as well be wearing the sunglasses.

Talk about bad farts. We avoid each other the rest of the afternoon. When my shift ends at three, I grab my sweater and hurry out the door.

While I'm waiting for the bus, I check my cell phone. Three

missed messages. I'm kind of hoping one will be from the Professor, but they're all from Tonya.

"Come over, okay?" says the last one. "I really need to talk to you."

Tonya's stretched out on the living room couch with her dreads tucked under the hood of her sweatshirt and a can of Mountain Dew in her hand. Her face is even paler than usual.

She doesn't know how close I came to blowing her off, after what she did to me at the party. But since I can count my friends on the fingers of one hand, I figure it will be easier to make up with her now than hang out by myself all summer. Not to mention that her brother's tight with the Professor.

"You look like crap, girl," I tell her.

She gives a weak smile. "You should've seen me this morning. Let's just say for a while there, the toilet bowl was my best friend."

"Tell me about it."

"I skipped school so I could get this place cleaned up before Mike gets home tonight."

She hasn't made much progress. Bottles and plastic cups cover every square inch of the coffee table, potato chip crumbs litter the floor, and an overflowing ashtray balances on the arm of the couch.

"You think this is bad, you should see the kitchen."

I plop down next to her. The soles of her white socks are gray, and her feet stink. I can pretty much predict what's going to happen: She'll say she's sorry forty-nine million times, and on the fifty-millionth time I'll forgive her.

"Come on," I say, "let's get it over with."

"Get what over with?"

"You know: 'I'm sorry, I'll never do it again,' and all that."

She sits up. "But I am sorry. Really, really sorry. I didn't mean to tell Laura, but I was majorly drunk and it sort of came out. I won't do it again, I promise."

"That's what you said last time."

"What can I say? I'm a screwup."

She looks so miserable with her shoulders sagging and the hood of her sweatshirt hiding her face that I feel my anger start to fade a little. I know she wasn't trying to hurt me; she just wanted to impress Laura. And if spreading stories about my bad fart of a life is the only way she can impress somebody, you've got to feel sorry for her.

But I decide to make her sweat a little. "I don't know if I can forgive you this time."

She takes a swig of her Mountain Dew. We both stare at the floor. I'm about to say something—maybe crack a joke to break the tension—when Doug bursts into the room in grass-stained gray sweats, hugging a football under one arm.

He points to the coffee table. "You better get this place picked up, or Mike's going to be pissed."

"I don't see you doing anything," Tonya says.

He grins and holds up the football. "Got to go to practice. Have fun."

"Loser!" Tonya shouts.

Doug wiggles his eyebrows at me. "That Prof is one crazy dude." Then he leaves, slamming the front door behind him.

I look at Tonya and shrug. If anyone's crazy, it's Doug.

"I'll help you clean up," I say.

Her face brightens for the first time. "Really?"

"Yeah." I get up and snag a couple of plastic cups. "You got a garbage bag or something?"

"Does this mean you forgive me, then?"

"I'm thinking about it."

We tour the house together, her holding the bag and me tossing in cups, bottles, and cigarette butts. Then we head out to the backyard and start clearing stuff off the deck. Even though it's cool, a late-afternoon sun peeks through the clouds, and Tonya ditches her sweatshirt.

"My brother's such a royal pain." She holds up an empty beer can like it's a football. " 'Gotta go to practice.' What a jerk."

I go long on the lawn. "Hey, throw me a pass."

She shakes the dregs of beer onto the grass and then heaves the can at me. I actually catch it. "Go for a touchdown!" she shouts.

I start running for the deck, but she tackles me and I tumble to the ground. We roll around a little, shoving each other and laughing. I sit up and pull some blades of dry grass out of my hair.

"You're not supposed to tackle your own team," I tell her.

She shrugs and laughs. "Who says I play by NFL rules?"

It takes us about an hour to finish cleaning up, and by the time we're done, the house looks better than I've ever seen it. We even reorganize Mike's collection of country CDs, alphabetically by artist.

"I think we're covered," Tonya says. "Let's go down to my room."

I've always been jealous of Tonya's bedroom. It's in the basement, and it's got a sparkly ceiling and its own tiny bathroom, just like a Motel 6. We sprawl out on her bed and prop ourselves up on her pillows. The pillowcases smell a little like greasy hair, but I pretend not to notice.

"So," Tonya says once she's settled, "I heard Cole was all over you last night."

"According to who?"

"According to Doug. He also told me the Professor gave you a ride home." She looks over at me. "So, spill it already. Did you guys end up in the back seat or what?"

"Like I'm going to tell you."

"Come on, I won't tell anybody, I promise."

"Yeah, right."

"Okay, fine, be that way." She grabs her laptop and logs on to Facebook. I peer over her shoulder; she's making a comment on Laura's wall.

"So what's the deal? You're hanging out with Laura now?"

She shrugs. "Sort of."

Then I get an idea. "Hey, look up Alan Parker."

Her face screws up like she sucked a lemon. "Alan Parker? What for?"

"Just look him up, okay?"

She tries a bunch of different searches, but we can't find him.

"Maybe he has a screen name," I say.

"I'd vote for Butt Wipe."

"Come on, he's not that bad. He works at that bird place I told you about—you know, where I've been volunteering—and he's actually kind of cool."

"Are you serious? The guy is *mean*. Remember how he used to hassle Gina?"

Gina was this special ed kid who smiled at everybody and wore glasses that made her eyes look too big for her face. Alan used to trip her every chance he got, and once he taped a note to her back that said, "Kick me, I'm stupid." Her parents finally transferred her to another school.

"And you know that thing he wrote all over the building? About Jeff Taylor?"

"Yeah." I can still see the words *Jeff Taylor is a faggot* scrawled across the front of the school in three-foot-high letters.

"Well, Jeff Taylor really was a faggot. I mean, he's gay. His parents are, like, born-agains or something, and when he saw his thing for guys advertised all over the school like that, he tried to kill himself. That's why Alan doesn't go to Ballard High anymore, in case you didn't know."

Her words sink to the bottom of my gut like a day-old doughnut. I always knew Alan had a mean streak a mile wide. But it's hard to believe the guy she's talking about is the same guy who taught me how to make a baby bird gape.

"You should see him with those birds, though."

"You think he really gives a rip about a bunch of birds? I bet he's just stuck there, doing community service. Don't kid yourself. Guys like him never change."

I pretend to agree with her, but inside I'm not so sure. Even though he jerked me around earlier, what sticks in my mind are those few minutes when he actually kidded with me and how he pretended to be a mother jay.

We give up searching for Alan on Facebook. Tonya shuts down her computer.

"Hey, want to try something?" she says. She digs around under her mattress and holds up a little plastic bag with a couple of blue pills in it. "Laura says they're awesome."

"What are they?"

"Her boyfriend's ADD medication. They're supposed to get you really wired. If we like them, she can get us some more."

"Here, let me see those."

She hands me the bag, and I shake the pills into my hand. They're so small and light and such a pretty Easter-egg blue, it's hard to imagine they could do much damage. I bring them close to my face and sniff. They don't smell like medicine. In fact they don't smell like anything at all.

"Go ahead, take one. It'll be fun."

I could definitely use a little fun. And Tonya and I have sort of been drifting apart lately; maybe this would be a way to get back with her again. I pinch a pill between my fingers and bring it to my lips, but I can't make myself open my mouth and stick it inside.

"Come on, take it already."

I flash on an image of Mom in Drake's window, with her too-thin face and shaking hands. I drop the pill back in the bag. "I don't think so."

"Fine. Then I will."

I see the look on Mom's face while she waits for Drake to set her up with a line. Still clutching the bag, I push myself off the bed. "What are you, insane?"

"What the—?"

"You don't even know what this stuff is. What if it really screws you up?"

"Give them here."

She reaches for the bag, but I hold it over my head. "No way."

She grabs at my T-shirt. "Give them here, Stevie!"

I jerk away and dash into the bathroom. She's right behind me, so I shake the bag over the stained toilet bowl and flush the pills down before she can stop me.

"What did you do that for?"

"Because I'm your friend. And you should stay away from Laura, because she's not." I toss the empty bag at her.

"Oh, I get it," she says. "You're jealous."

I bark out a laugh. "Of that slut?"

"Don't you call my friend a slut."

"Try slutty whore, then."

She narrows her eyes and gives me the finger. "Why don't you just get the hell out of here?"

"Fine." I leave her standing in her smelly bathroom and make for the stairs without looking back.

It's around five, so traffic is crazy. I have plenty of time to sit in the back of the packed bus and go over what happened. I've had fights with Tonya before, but nothing like this. Ever since she started hanging out with Laura, it's like I hardly know her.

By the time I get off the bus downtown for my transfer, the fact that I haven't eaten is starting to catch up with me. I hit the McDonald's on Third Avenue and order a Quarter Pounder with extra cheese. While I'm chowing down, I decide a movie might get my mind off things, so when I'm finished I hike over to Pacific Place and buy a ticket for some stupid movie I've seen previews for on TV. It's a total waste of money, because all I can do is sit there and think about Tonya and Mom and those little blue pills and crystal meth.

I get back to Aunt Mindy's about ten-thirty. I'm dying of thirst after that Quarter Pounder, so I head into the kitchen and pour myself a big glass of OJ. Juice splashes onto the counter. Of course Aunt Mindy picks that exact moment to shuffle into the room in her robe and slippers.

"I hope you were planning to clean that up," she says. She tries to hand me a sponge. "And by the way, it's after ten. Where have you been?"

I turn away. "Don't even start, okay? I had a fight with my best friend, and I miss Mom and I'm not going to see her all summer, and . . ." I can't get anything else out past the knot in my throat.

Her frown disintegrates. "Oh, sweetie, I'm sorry. What was I thinking? Of course this is hard for you. It's hard for me too." She hugs me from behind. Her bathrobe is nubby against my arms. I close my eyes and just for a moment, I imagine it's Mom holding me.

Then she says, "But I'm not going to put up with you disappearing like that. Next time at least call and let me know where you are."

I unwind her arms and step away. I can't pretend anymore. She's so not Mom.

CHAPTER 10

Hi Mom,

It's me, Stevie. Sorry I didn't write sooner, but I was pretty sure you were mad at me for talking to Aunt Mindy. Believe me, most of the time I wish I'd kept my big mouth shut. I mean, I'm the one who has to put up with her for the whole summer now. But it will be worth it if you get better.

She says the place you're in is nice and that it's real close to the ocean. Can you hear the waves from your room? I know you'd love that. But I hope you don't love it too much, cuz I definitely want you to come back!

When you get home, let's make popcorn with extra butter and watch WWE Smackdown. I could never do that with Aunt Mindy. She'd have a heart attack if I got butter on her precious white couch. Plus she likes to watch Great Performances on PBS (gag!).

I miss you, Mom. Write soon so I know you're OK and that you're not mad at me.

Love,
Stevie

I read the letter aloud. It took me over an hour to write, but it still sounds like something a third-grader would come up with. I think about ripping it up and starting over, but I've already done that four times and it didn't help. Besides, it's been two weeks since Mom left for rehab, and I can't see waiting much longer. So I fold the lined paper, making sharp creases with my fingernails, and slip it under my pillow.

Aunt Mindy left for work hours ago, but the smell of her coffee haunts the house. Outside the guest room window, puffy clouds hover in the sky and the Olympic Mountains peek over the evergreens. A crow caws from a nearby telephone wire.

My cell phone rings. I'm thinking maybe it's Tonya calling to say she's sorry, but it's the Professor. Even though I know he can't see me, I suck in my stomach and run my fingers through my hair.

"Hey," I say, "where'd you get my number?"

He laughs. "I have my sources."

It had to be Tonya, since she's the only one who knows it besides Aunt Mindy. I wonder if she told him about our fight or the blue pills, but I'm not about to ask.

"What's up?" I say.

"A couple of us are heading down to Carkeek Park. Want to come?"

I glance at the clock. I'm supposed to meet Rick at the library in twenty minutes. Thrillsville. We've been meeting for three weeks now, and I still don't know what he's talking about half the time. And of course, I still haven't done that book report.

"What time are you leaving?" I ask.

"Like, right now. I could swing by and pick you up in, say, ten minutes."

I imagine a day of hanging out in the park, of gazing into the

Professor's eyes and maybe getting back to the kiss we started after Tonya's party. I'm tempted to ditch Rick and go for it, but the hell I'd catch from Aunt Mindy wouldn't be worth it.

"Can't," I say. "But maybe I could meet up with you guys later."

I hear laughter in the background, and then a girl's voice says, "Let's get a move on, Prof." It sounds a lot like Laura Rogers, but there's no way he'd hang out with her.

"Which side of the park are you going to?" I ask.

"Come on!" the girl says again. I could swear it's Laura.

He laughs. "I'm getting yelled at here. Catch you later, okay?"

I toss my cell phone onto the bed. It isn't fair. I'm the only kid in Seattle who has to spend summer vacation in the friggin' library. But I tell myself I'd rather do a thousand book reports than hang out with Laura or even Tonya right now. I just don't get why a smart guy like the Professor would want to hang with them, either.

In an effort to shake off my stinky mood, I throw on my camouflage pants and an orange crop top. Just for fun I shove my feet into a pair of red heels so high I feel like I'm on stilts. On my way to the library, some old dude with a cowboy hat leans out his car window and yells, "Hey, babe, need a ride?" I mouth "No," but I smile at him, like Mom would. The high heels pinch my toes. Amazingly I manage to make it to the library without tripping and breaking my neck.

Rick strolls into the conference room. He has a new, super-short haircut, and the little stubble of beard that used to pepper his chin is gone. He glances at my shoes, then smiles and shakes his head. "Did you get a chance to look at those math problems I gave you?"

"Um . . . actually, I was pretty busy."

He raises one eyebrow. "I won't even ask you about the book report, then. I know all about busy weekends."

No doubt. I bet he got his hair cut to impress some hot date.

"We'll just go over those problems together, then."

He's reaching for my math book when I notice the pieces of paper sticking out between the pages. My latest NTD House drawings! Before I can do anything about it, he's opening one of the papers and smoothing it on the table.

"What's this?"

"Nothing." I reach out to snatch it away.

He anchors the paper to the table with his hand and studies it. "Very cool. It reminds me of an architectural drawing."

It *is* one of my better ones. I spent hours putting in lots of detail—a spiral staircase and a skylight and everything. Still, having him stare at my NTD House—which no one besides Mom knows about—is kind of driving me insane. I try to pull the paper out from under his hand, but he presses down harder.

"I thought we were doing math."

He looks at me, then back at the drawing. "Okay, let's do some math." He jabs his finger in the middle of my living room. "What's the slope of this skylight?"

"How should I know?"

"I'll tell you how you should know." He opens my notebook and starts scribbling. I've never seen him this excited before. "You use the mathematical formula for determining slope."

I stare at his chicken scratches. "I'm not really into numbers."

"But let's say you're talking to the contractor who's going to build this house. How's he going to get that skylight just the way you want it if you don't know the slope? How's he going to build that beautiful spiral staircase without knowing the dimensions of each stair? And how's he going to come in on budget without an estimate of the cost of materials? It's all about numbers, Stevie."

"Okay, okay, I get it."

We spend the next half hour figuring out the square footage of each room, the slope of the skylight, the dimensions of the staircase. It's actually kind of fun, and by the time we're done, I've scribbled numbers all over my drawing.

I figure we'll drop the whole thing when we get to Language Arts, but no, he has me write a paragraph describing the house using simile and metaphor. We go through all the subjects like that, relating everything to my NTD House. When he closes the books and tells me it's three o'clock, I can hardly believe it.

He winks at me. "Like they say, time flies when you're having fun."

I roll my eyes the way I always do when he says something corny, but I'm actually bummed we have to quit.

"I'm glad we finally found it, Stevie."

"Found what?"

"Something you can get excited about. I knew it was there somewhere." He stuffs his books into his bag, and I can't help noticing the ripple of muscles under his shirt.

"They're just drawings."

"Don't sell yourself short. You've got a great sense of space and design. You could be an architect someday if you wanted. Ever think of that?"

I shake my head.

He looks at me for a long time. "The future's going to get here whether you think about it or not. You could do it, Stevie. If you studied hard and got yourself to college, you could make drawings like that and get paid for it."

I concentrate on the little dents my heels are making in the beige carpet. I just figured when I graduate, I'll get a job as a waitress or something. Or help Mom with her jewelry business.

He looks down, then looks back at me and clears his throat. "Maybe it's not my place to say this, but while we're on the subject of your future, you might want to rethink the way you're dressing. Personally, I like your look. But you wouldn't want to show up at a job interview dressed like that."

I wrap my arms around my naked middle to shut out the sting of his words. Who does he think he is, anyway? I know I dress different; that's what me and Mom do. Aunt Mindy's always offering to take me shopping, but I refuse to go.

"What's it to you?"

"Hey, no need to get bent out of shape. I'm just saying you got to start taking yourself seriously, girl. If you don't, nobody else will. And you deserve to be taken seriously. You really do."

I stare at him. Nobody's ever told me I could go to college. And for sure nobody's told me I deserve to be taken seriously. It seems like the kind of stuff a dad would say.

Not that I would know. The only thing I know about my dad is his name was Eddie and he left before I was born. I wish he was still around, though. If I had a dad, I bet Mom wouldn't be working at the club. She wouldn't stay out all night, and she wouldn't be into drugs. If I had a dad, I wouldn't have to keep her away from Drake.

"Uh-oh," Rick says. "You know I didn't mean to hurt your feelings."

I fake a smile. "Allergies."

A week goes by and I don't hear from Mom. I check the mailbox every day, but it's always stuffed with bills and catalogs for Aunt

Mindy. I tell myself Mom's busy or maybe they don't let her write letters.

Then on Saturday morning I'm cracking open one eyelid, checking to see if it's noon yet, when there's a knock on the guest room door.

"Stevie," says Aunt Mindy, "mail for you."

I jump out of bed and throw open the door. Aunt Mindy's wearing black spandex shorts and a sports bra, and she's got a flowered gardening glove on her left hand. In her right hand she's holding an envelope. Even from across the room, I can tell the handwriting on it is Mom's.

It's weird: I've been waiting forever for this letter, but the thought of actually opening it makes me so nervous I could puke.

She looks at me and frowns. "You want me to read it to you?"

I nod.

"I planted your mom's hydrangea in the front yard, next to my azalea," she says as she gets rid of the glove and then perches on the edge of the bed. "They can keep each other company."

I plop down next to her; she smells like plants and dirt. She slits the envelope open and slides out a folded sheet of paper. It's the kind with blue lines, like you tear out of a notebook. I want to tell her to hurry, but it's hard to talk when you're not breathing.

"Hey, Honey Pie," she reads.

I can imagine Mom giving me a squeeze as she says this. I can even imagine her smell and the feel of her arms around me.

Aunt Mindy looks up. "You want me to keep going?"

I can't talk through the tears I'm choking back, so I just nod.

"Got your letter. Sorry it took me so long to write back. They keep me busy around here. I'm not mad at you. I'm the one that screwed up.

"My counselor here helps me understand stuff about my life. Like

that I've been a crappy mom. Being a good little prisoner (ha ha), so they'll let me out of here early.

"P.S. Soon as I get back, let's do a Smackdown party—popcorn with extra butter. I promise you things will be different."

Aunt Mindy folds the paper real slow and sticks it back in the envelope. "I'm glad she answered your letter. Be careful, though. I don't want to see you get hurt."

"What's that supposed to mean?"

She sighs. "How can I put this? I'd take it with a grain of salt if I were you—all that business about things being different. I'm sure she means well, but people don't change overnight."

I look at her like she's gone crazy. "You saying my mom's a liar?"

"June always has lots of big ideas, but she can be skimpy on the follow-through."

Great. Right when I'm starting to think Aunt Mindy might not be that bad, she goes and pulls this your-mom's-a-loser crap again.

I stand. "Like you're so perfect."

"All I'm saying is, your mom hasn't got much of a track record."

"Quit talking bad about her."

She gets up to leave and holds out the envelope. "I don't want you to get your hopes up and—"

"Shut your face!" I snatch the letter from her hand and flop onto the bed. "I hate you!"

CHAPTER 11

I avoid Aunt Mindy the next few days, which is easy. There's some big workshop going on at the Pilates studio, and she has to be there from early morning until, like, eight at night. Mostly she leaves notes: *I won't be home for dinner, there's leftover chicken in the fridge* or *Here's three dollars, pick up some milk* or *Don't forget the recycling.* I rip them into tiny pieces.

I start spending even more time at On the Wing. Every day I hop the bus over there as soon as Aunt Mindy leaves and stay till it's time for tutoring or till Valerie forces me to go home. No matter how pissed I am at Aunt Mindy, hanging out with the birds always calms me down.

I'm heading to On the Wing Wednesday morning when it starts to rain. If there's one thing I hate about Seattle, it's the weather. Winters are bad enough—the weather's cold and wet, but at least it's predictable. Summers, though, are all over the place. You'll get a stretch of eighty-five-degree days, and you'll think you can finally put your winter stuff into storage. Then the next morning you wake up and it's sixty degrees and raining.

But today it's not just raining, it's pouring. I hang my hoodie on the hook by the back door and wander into the cage room, where a chocolaty aroma hangs in the air.

"Smells awesome in here," I say to Alan, who's leaning against the counter. I'm still pissed at him, but I figure since we have to work together, I should at least try to be civil.

He holds up a mug with a picture of a German shepherd on it. "Hot chocolate. Want some?"

"Sure."

I study his back as he microwaves me some hot water. "It's just us today. Valerie's visiting her sister in Sequim."

He hands me a mug and a packet of Swiss Miss, and I'm careful not to let our hands touch. I take my first swallow too fast; it scorches my lips and burns all the way down to my belly.

"Watch out," he says, "it's hot." He gives me one of those straight-ahead smiles.

"Well, we'd better start feeding," I say, glad of an excuse to turn away. I don't know why he's being so nice all of a sudden. I pull on a latex glove, then take a yogurt cup out of the warmer and set it on a plastic tray, along with a syringe, a paintbrush, a paper cup filled with water, and a wad of cotton balls. "I'll start with the baskets."

I always volunteer to do the baskets, now that Tweety Bird has graduated from her incubator. As soon as I lift the net cover off the first basket, the crows inside start to gape and caw, opening their beaks so wide I can practically see into their stomachs.

"Hi, guys," I whisper. I glance at Alan to make sure he doesn't hear me talking to the birds, but he's busy at the incubators. A couple of swipes along the crows' tongues with a paintbrush dipped in water, and they're ready for the syringe. They jockey for position as I go back and forth between them, injecting brown mush down their wide-open beaks.

I know I shouldn't hurry, but I'm anxious to get to Tweety Bird. So I give the crows a quick bath with the mister and then replace the basket cover. I continue down the line, feeding a fat jay, two tiny bushtits, and a couple of swallows. At last I come to the blue basket labeled "American Robin D."

"Hey, Tweety girl," I whisper as I set down the feeding tray and fill a syringe. But when I lift the net, the basket is empty. I stare at the bare perch as if looking hard enough could make her reappear.

Alan comes up behind me. "Oh, yeah, I forgot to tell you. We moved the robin to the aviary. I haven't gotten around to cleaning out the basket yet."

What do you mean, 'the robin'? That's Tweety Bird! I want to say. But I know he'd just make fun of me. "When was that?" I ask.

"Yesterday after you left. It's still eating formula, but it's also been eating some dish food and flapping its wings a lot, so we decided it was ready. We can keep syringe-feeding it in the aviary till it's completely weaned."

"Thanks a lot." I slam the syringe down so hard the water cup tips over. Water spills onto the feeding tray; the cotton balls are a soggy mess.

"Whoa, what's your problem?"

"You could have waited for me. She is my bird."

"Just because you found it doesn't mean it's—"

"You know what I mean."

He peels off his glove. "Come on. Let's go take a look."

I grab my hoodie and follow him out the back door. The rain has let up some, and the drops feel like tiny pins pricking my skin. Our shoes make sucking sounds as we traipse across the wet lawn. I haven't spent much time in the aviaries, which are like giant, walk-in birdcages. For one thing, they make me kind of nervous: birds flying all over the place and pooping on you or sitting on the ground where you could squish them with one wrong step. For another thing, the aviary is the last place a bird goes before you have to say goodbye to it for good.

We get close to the first aviary and peek in. Birds flit from branch to branch, sometimes swooping down to eat soaked cat chow, worms, or berries from the food dish on the floor.

He points to a branch near the aviary ceiling. "There it is."

It's Tweety Bird all right. She's perched there, puffing out her sleek, spotted belly like she's trying to show it off. I can hardly believe she's the same pathetic bird I spotted near the cemetery just over a month ago.

I unlatch the aviary door and let myself in. The air smells like fresh leaves and bird poop. I move slowly to the branch where Tweety Bird sits.

"Hey, Tweety," I call, not caring what Alan thinks anymore.

She just looks at me through one beady black eye.

"Come here, girl."

I reach toward her, but she sidesteps to the other end of the branch.

"Come on, Tweety, it's me!"

She takes off, flitting to a branch at the opposite side of the aviary.

I can't keep my voice from breaking. "Stupid bird!"

Next thing I know, Alan's beside me. "Look," he says, "I told you not to get attached."

The rain picks up again, and fat drops fall through the aviary roof. I shiver and pull my hoodie tight around me.

"You cold?" He takes off his army jacket and puts it over my shoulders.

I'm surprised how gentle his touch is. For some reason I'm scared to look at him.

"How can you stand it?" I ask. "How can you stand to start caring about them and then have to let them go?"

He shrugs. "You get used to it after a while."

I remember what Tonya said, about him only working here because he has to. "You do care about them, right?"

"What's that supposed to mean?"

"This friend of mine thought you were only doing this because you have to, for community service."

He stiffens. "Don't you and your friends have anything better to talk about?"

Why does he have to turn every single thing I say into something negative? I try again. "I told her when you're with the birds, you're cool. I mean, you're patient with them. And, well, sort of gentle."

"Great. Now she probably thinks I'm a fairy."

I have to laugh at that one. "Give me a break. I'm trying to say something nice."

He turns away. I usually think of Alan as this big guy. But when I see him standing there, his shoulders hunched against the cold, he looks more like a sad little kid. I never noticed before that his dark hair has hints of red in it.

"I also told her that inside, I think you're a good person."

For a minute the only sound is the flitting of bird wings. Then he turns back to me, still staring at the muddy ground, and says, "Yeah, right. Like you actually believe that."

"Yeah," I tell him, "I actually do."

He looks up, and I feel like I'm falling into his eyes. I'm not sure who starts it, but suddenly we're kissing. His strong arms wrap around my back. His face is clammy and cold, but his lips are warm. He covers my mouth with tiny, soft kisses. I start to pull away, then realize I want more. He cradles the back of my head, holding me gently as his kisses get longer and deeper. I let my mouth open beneath his.

But as soon as his tongue touches mine, I twist away. What am I thinking? I've got a chance with the Professor, and I'm not about to screw that up for Alan Parker.

"What's wrong?"

"I've gotta go." I thrust his wet jacket at him, burst through the aviary door, and take off across the spongy lawn.

"Wait!" he yells.

But I just keep going.

CHAPTER 12

When I was a kid, I made mud sundaes. I'd turn the hose on some dirt, mush it up real good, and then slop it into a plastic cup. That was the ice cream. Then I'd dribble more mud on top for the chocolate sauce. Next came some dry grass—the sprinkles—and last of all a rock for the cherry on top.

My life right now is like one of those sundaes. Mom being in rehab? That's the pile of mud. The hassles with Aunt Mindy are the grass, and now the weirdness with Alan is the rock sitting on top of the whole mess.

I haven't seen him since last week, but I can't seem to get him off my mind. I'll be dreaming about the Professor, and all of a sudden it's Alan I'm kissing. Then, right in the middle of it, he turns back into the Professor again, and all I want to do is get away from both of them. I decide the only sane thing to do is stay clear of Alan for a few days. I feel lousy for lying, but I call Valerie and tell her I've got the flu.

Only problem is, if I don't hang out at On the Wing, I've got no excuse to avoid Aunt Mindy. It's been over a week since our fight, and I'm still mad at her for talking bad about Mom. I have to live with the woman the rest of the summer, though, so I wish I could rewind the whole scene and erase the part where I said I hated her. Lying in bed on Wednesday morning, I decide as soon as she gets home from work, I'm going to tell her I'm sorry.

She beats me to it. When I drag myself out of bed at eleven and shuffle into the kitchen to see if she's left any coffee, I find a note waiting for me on the table. *Stevie,* it says, *I surrender. I'm getting off early. Let's go shopping.*

I haven't been to Northgate Mall in like a million years—it's the kind of place Mom wouldn't be caught dead in. But after Rick's lecture about my clothes, this time I decide to take Aunt Mindy up on her invitation. Plus I'm hoping a shopping trip will give me a chance to patch things up with her.

I have to admit it's kind of fun taking it all in: the dorky mall walkers in their matching tracksuits and blinding white cross-trainers; the snotty-nosed kids dragging their moms into Toys R Us; the smell of popcorn, Starbucks coffee, and cinnamon rolls.

"Let's start at Macy's," Aunt Mindy says. She wants to buy me a new "outfit." With her taste in clothes, this could be scary. We take the elevator up to the junior department, where they've got techno music playing so loud the floor throbs.

She homes in on a faceless mannequin in low-rise jeans and a T-shirt the color of strawberry ice cream. "Isn't that adorable? You'd look so cute in that."

The getup is so generic I could gag, but I try it on to make her happy. When I come out of the dressing room with price tags dangling, she gazes at me like I'm a bride showing off her wedding dress. "Oh, sweetie, that's darling."

I study myself in the full-length mirror and decide there's a good reason I never wear pink.

I veto everything in Macy's junior department, so she drags me into another store. And another. And another. Just when I've decided that if I have to try on one more so-called cute outfit I'll keel over and die, she halts in front of a shop window and points. "Look, Stevie. It's you."

The mannequin is posed in a position no human being could actually get into, with her legs too far apart and her arms stretched behind her back. But it's what she's wearing that gets my attention: a pair of tight gray denim pants with pockets outlined in white stitching and a black top that shows a triangle of skin under one side of her collarbone.

Aunt Mindy grabs my arm and pulls me into the store. "You're trying it on."

For once I don't argue. I tell the saleslady my size and slip into the dressing room she starts for me. I try the pants on first. Perfect: tight enough to show off my butt, but not so tight I can't sit down. Then I put on the top, and I'm in love. It looks even better on me than it did on the mannequin. It hugs my boobs but doesn't make them look too big, and the triangle hits me just right, so the strap of my black lace bra peeks through.

I can't wipe the grin off my face when I come out to show Aunt Mindy. She claps and says, "Let's get you some shoes to go with it."

By the time we leave the shoe store, I'm feeling lightheaded. I've got a bag with the pants and top in it under one arm and a shoebox with a pair of chunky-heeled clogs under the other. I can hardly believe the amount of money Aunt Mindy signed for on her credit card without guilt-tripping me once.

When I stop at the window of Body Jewelry Plus to look at belly button rings, she says, "Go ahead and browse for a while if you want. I need to pop into JCPenney." She glances at her watch. "I'll meet you at the Starbucks in the food court in, say, twenty minutes."

I've snagged a table along the far wall and am halfway through my caramel latte by the time Aunt Mindy arrives. She hustles over carrying a JCPenney shopping bag. When she sets it down on the table, I peek inside.

"What'd you get?"

"Nothing interesting. Just socks and underwear." She takes the bag from me and stows it under her chair, but not before I catch sight of something small, black, and lacy.

I'm tempted to give her a hard time, but she just spent a couple hundred bucks on me. "Thanks for the clothes," I say instead, swiping up the foam that's stuck to the sides of my cup. "They're awesome."

"My pleasure. It was fun."

There's some kind of jazz music playing, saxophone and drums. I keep time by tapping the bottom of my cup against the table. I know I'm stalling. Finally the song ends.

"I'm sorry," I say. "About the other day. I shouldn't have said that."

"I'm sorry too. I shouldn't have said anything against your mom. I only wish she . . . Never mind. I'll quit while I'm ahead." She sticks out her hand. "Truce?"

I shake it. "Truce."

There's not much to say after that, so she finishes her mocha in silence. I pretend to be lost in an article about all-ages clubs in *The Stranger*.

She sets down her cup, fishes the bag from under her chair, and slings her purse strap over her shoulder. "You ready to get out of here?"

I make a show of needing to finish the last paragraph. "Sure."

I follow her out of the mall, watching her hips sway under her skirt. I'm sure that lacy black thing was a thong, and now it's impossible to erase from my mind the ridiculous picture of it riding up her crack.

A couple of days go by. I know I can't stay away from Alan forever, so one morning I jump the bus back to the old neighborhood. But the closer I get to On the Wing, the less ready I feel to face him. I decide to get off at 8th and 85th and walk for a while, give myself some time to figure things out.

It's a perfect day for the way I'm feeling. The sky is heavy and gray, and mist clings to the tops of the evergreens. The gas-station-attendant's shirt I've got on over my tank barely keeps out the chill. A skinny guy with a ponytail lounging in front of the Sundown Tavern waves his cigarette at me as I pass. The smoke burns my nose and makes me think of Mom. I wander over to our apartment. Well, it's not really ours anymore. They evicted us when Mom went to rehab since she didn't pay the rent. Aunt Mindy didn't pay it either. She thinks we can find a better place when Mom gets back, and she had our stuff put in storage.

I stand and stare at the white Corolla with bird poop on the back windshield that sits in Mom's old parking spot. If it wasn't for me, we'd be together in the apartment right now. But wishing isn't going to change anything, so I turn away, pass the Chevron station and the McDonald's and take a right onto Holman Road.

Traffic whizzes by, leaving a haze of stinky exhaust. A couple of cars honk at me, but I don't bother to look up. I don't know how far I've walked—miles, probably—and I can feel the beginning of a blister on my left heel. It starts to sprinkle as I cross 3rd and then Greenwood and finally hang a right on Aurora, home of used car lots and sleazy motels.

As I walk I go round and round in my head. Should I tell Alan about the Professor? I haven't heard from him since the day I turned down his invite to the beach, so I'm starting to wonder if there's anything to tell. Why hasn't he called me? And what would I do if Alan tried to kiss me again?

I'm so lost in thought I almost don't notice the crow lying on its side in the corner of a parking lot. As I get closer, it struggles to drag itself a few inches along the asphalt, panic in its beady eyes. One wing sticks out at a weird angle.

I kneel beside it. "It's okay, little guy. I'll take care of you." Then I strip off my shirt and gather the crow inside. Alan or no Alan, I've got to get this bird to Valerie.

It feels like a million miles to On the Wing. Rain soaks the shirt in my hands, and the crow inside it is so still I'm starting to wonder if it's dead. By the time I finally get there, my teeth are chattering.

Even though I can't wait to get out of the rain, I hesitate outside the back door. Then I feel the crow struggle underneath the shirt, and I know I have no choice. I open the door and step into the cage room.

The birds greet me with squawks and chirps, but I don't see Alan anywhere. Valerie's not around either. I stand in the middle of the room, holding the crow and shivering, not sure what to do.

Then I hear voices from the living room. One is Valerie's, the other I don't recognize.

"He could definitely present some challenges for you," the unfamiliar voice says.

I tiptoe into the kitchen and peek through the half-open doorway. Valerie's sitting at the dining room table opposite a big lady with long, dark hair and too much makeup.

"I don't know how much you know about his background," the lady says. "This kid has moved around a lot."

Valerie must be taking on a new volunteer. I squeeze closer to the doorway so I can hear and see better.

The lady reaches into her briefcase and pulls out some papers. "These are the reports from the families who have fostered him. They all cite angry outbursts and incidents of cruelty as reasons for terminating care. It's going to require a lot of patience to take him on."

Valerie takes the papers but doesn't look at them. "He's had a hard life, but he's a wonderful young man," she says. "I've seen plenty evidence of that here. What he needs is a stable home, and I believe I can provide that for him. He's been unofficially living here for the past few months, anyway."

They must be talking about Alan! I squeeze even closer.

"We appreciate that you're willing to take in an older teenager. Most people want babies, or at least little kids. But the older ones need just as much love and care. Maybe more, sometimes. So many of them get pushed out of the foster-care system the day they turn eighteen and end up homeless or in jail. Or worse."

"I've heard that. And that's the last thing I'd want for him."

The lady smiles. "We know you have a unique relationship with Alan, so we're hopeful the adoption process can go smoothly."

She's adopting him? I back up so fast I bump a china teacup off the counter. It hits the floor and smashes to bits.

"What was that?" the lady says.

Still cradling the crow in one arm, I drop to the floor and hurry to gather up the pieces.

Valerie rushes into the kitchen. "Stevie! Are you okay?"

I know my face must be turning a million shades of red. "I'm sorry. I'll buy you another one."

"I don't care about the cup." She pulls me to my feet and looks me up and down. "Oh, honey, you're soaked. You shouldn't be out in this weather, especially with the flu."

I hold out the shirt. "I came to bring you this crow. I think it's hurt pretty bad."

"Everything okay?" calls the lady from the living room.

Valerie pokes her head around the doorway. "Fine. But can we finish up another time? I've got a bit of a situation here."

She takes the bundle from me as gently as if she's picking up a baby. "Now, young lady, let's get you out of those wet things. There's a robe hanging on my bedroom door. Change into that, and we'll put your clothes in the dryer."

When I come back to the cage room hugging my wad of wet clothes, Valerie's got the crow laid out on the old wooden desk she uses for an examining table. She pulls on a pair of latex gloves and peels away the shirt like she's unwrapping a fragile Christmas present.

The crow just lies there. Only the rise and fall of its chest tells me it's still alive.

"I hope I didn't hurt it."

"You did a great job." She turns it over, running her hands along its drooping wing. "But I'm not sure there's much we can do."

"You can fix it. You fix all the other birds."

She touches the wing again and shakes her head. "I'll do everything I possibly can, but it's in pretty bad shape. You shouldn't get your hopes up." She wrestles off the gloves. "The dryer's in the basement, right as you come down the stairs. While you're tossing your clothes in, I'll get this crow into a basket. I want to work on that wing later, but right now it needs dark and quiet."

I could use a little dark and quiet myself. I'm still trying to wrap my mind around what I overheard.

◆

"It's about lunchtime," Valerie says when we meet back in the kitchen. "Why don't you join me for some leftover chili?"

We take our steaming bowls to the little table in the living room, and Valerie shoves a stack of magazines aside. She hands me a sweaty can of Sprite. *"Bon appétit."*

We spoon up our chili for a few minutes in silence. It's rich and spicy, with little chunks of meat in it.

Finally I can't stand it anymore. "Are you really adopting Alan?"

She chuckles. "I was wondering how much of that conversation you heard."

"I didn't mean to. I—"

"That's okay. Yes, I've started the adoption process. He needs someone to love him. And since my son's been gone . . ." She picks up her can of Sprite but doesn't take a drink. I think about the photo in her bedroom, the boy with Valerie's eyes.

"The one with the baseball glove?"

She takes a deep breath and answers the question I don't know how to ask. "It was a small-plane crash. He and my husband were both killed."

"I'm sorry."

She looks up at me and smiles, but the smile never makes it to her eyes. "It was a long time ago. He was right around Alan's age when I lost him. So you see, I need Alan as much as he needs me."

I try to imagine what it would be like to have Valerie take care of me, and for a second I feel a twinge of jealousy. Then I shake it off. What do I have to be jealous about? I've still got Mom.

The Fourth of July is Mom's favorite holiday. Not because she's patriotic or anything—she just likes to set off fireworks. Last year was our first Fourth in Seattle, so we celebrated by buying a whole bunch of fireworks cheap, at one of those stands out on the reservation. Roman candles, sparklers, fountains—Mom bought them all.

We didn't know much of anybody back then, so we had our own little party in the alley behind the motel we were living in. We chugged a beer, then Mom set off the fireworks. I can still smell the gunpowder and see the way she waved her arms and whooped and cheered when those pretty colors lit up the night air. I was nervous she'd burn herself or the cops would hassle us. But looking back, I think of it as one of our top-ten good times.

So when I start hearing the boom and sizzle of fireworks Saturday night around eleven, I wish I could bring that good time back again. Aunt Mindy invited me to some barbeque, but I can't imagine hanging out with a bunch of people I don't know when the only person I really want to be with is Mom.

On Monday Aunt Mindy reminds me she's taking a couple of days off. Oh, joy. She has these big plans to plant a vegetable garden in the backyard. She's out there Tuesday afternoon in her shorts and sports bra, digging in the dirt, when I put on my new duds and head for the library.

Rick walks into the conference room and sets his bag on a table. "Let's see what you've got for me today."

I pull out my latest drawing, which is of a backyard with a swimming pool. He has me do a new drawing every week, and I'm definitely getting better at it. He makes me put in the measurements of everything now; I've gotten better at that too.

He leans over to study it. "Good work with your measurements. Now let's go over what you know about volume." He scoots his chair closer to mine. "You say here the swimming pool is ten by twenty-five feet, with a depth of five feet. Let's imagine the pool is empty, and you want to know how many gallons of water you'd need to fill it. You remember the formula I gave you last week?"

I nod. I'm really trying to pay attention, but I've just noticed that he's wearing a new cologne.

"So what's the length times the width times the depth?"

I look up at him. "Let me guess. You've got a new girlfriend, right?"

"Huh?"

"You know. The cologne. The haircut."

He laughs. "Now, hang on a second. We're here to talk about your education, not my love life." He taps the drawing with the eraser end of his pencil. "Have you come up with the answer yet?"

"So, who is she? Some Microsoft babe?"

He holds up both hands. "Whoa. Getting a little personal, aren't we? Let's get back to your drawing."

We work on volume equations for the rest of the session. When the time's up, he gives me my homework, and then I pack up my stuff.

"Have a good week with your new hottie," I say over my shoulder as I'm leaving, just to bug him. I expect him to tell me to give it a rest, but he doesn't say a word.

I turn around. I never saw a black guy turn red before, but I swear his cheeks are pink.

"Okay, Stevie. We were going tell you," he says.

For a second I stare at him. And then it all makes sense: the haircut, the new cologne.

The thong?

I read somewhere that seeing your parents have sex could damage you for life. Now I know that imagining your aunt doing it— especially with your tutor—is even worse.

"We should talk," he says, but I'm out the door. I take the long way back, trying to wrap my head around the whole thing.

I have to admit I sort of had this fantasy about Rick getting together with Mom. Not that I'm dumb enough to actually think it would work. But Mom really needs a guy like him, and I . . . *Forget it,* I tell myself. *Just file that one under "Things That Are Never Going to Happen."*

But the more I think about it, the more pissed I get. Aunt Mindy's got plenty of dough; what does she need a rich guy for? How come everything always works out so perfect for her, and nothing ever works out for me and Mom?

I expect to find Aunt Mindy in the backyard, but instead she's sitting at the kitchen table, staring into her coffee cup. I'm ready to spit out some snotty remark about her and Rick when she looks up and says, "Stevie. I'm glad you're home." She picks up her coffee cup and cradles it in her hands. "I spoke to your mom today."

My heart starts to race. "When?"

"She called about half an hour ago."

"What did she say?"

She looks at me and sighs. Her face is so sad, I'm thinking something awful must have happened.

"What did she say?" I ask again.

"She said she's had enough treatment. She wants to leave rehab."

The thought that we might be together again soon makes me so happy, I don't know whether to laugh or cry. "That's great!"

She shakes her head. "She's only been there six weeks, and it's a twelve-week program."

"But if she's better . . ."

"I know you want her to come home, sweetheart, but I don't think it's right."

Leave it to Aunt Mindy to ruin everything. I put my hands on my hips and glare at her. "Oh, I get it. You don't want her to come back and steal your boyfriend."

"What?"

"I know about you and Rick."

I can tell I've caught her off guard. Blood rushes to her face. "That has nothing to do with it. I only want her to finish the program. She asked me to loan her money for bus fare, but I said no."

My mouth drops open. "You've got to be kidding me."

She doesn't answer.

Fireworks go off in my gut. I give the table leg a good kick. "You think you're so hot with your Pilates and your fancy house and your rich boyfriend. What's the big frickin' deal if Mom has to borrow a few bucks of your precious money?"

"It's not about the money. But you're darn right my money's precious." She slams down her coffee cup and stands. "I work hard for that money—which is one thing I've sure as hell never seen your mom do."

I stare at her. "Oh, my God, you really do hate her, don't you?"

"How can you say that?"

"She always told me you hated her. Looks like she was right."

She pulls her "poor me" face, acts like she's all hurt. "That is so unfair. I'm only trying to do what's best for her."

She's such a fake that I actually have to laugh. "What a load of crap. All you ever think about is you."

"Oh, really? Well, let me tell you something. You want to know who doesn't care about anyone but herself?" She leans across the table and gets right in my face. "June Elizabeth Calhoun, that's who."

Nobody talks about Mom that way.

"Screw you!" I race to the guest room. *I wish I'd never come to live in this house.* I grab my old green overnight bag and start stuffing in clothes: my panties, bras, plaid boxers, and gypsy skirts. Beaded old-lady sweaters and lace shawls, men's flannel shirts and camouflage pants. *I wish I'd never seen Aunt Mindy's stupid thong.* Tanks, camis, midriffs, bikinis. Tight jeans, baggy jeans, faded jeans, embroidered jeans. I tear my stuff off every hanger and empty every drawer. *And more than anything in the world, I wish I'd never ratted on Mom.*

I zip my bag and sling it over my shoulder. On my way to the door, I notice Aunt Mindy's keys hanging on their hook. *Don't,* I tell myself. Then I hear the back door shut, so I run to the kitchen and peek through the blinds. Aunt Mindy's out in the yard, scowling as she jams her shovel into the dirt.

I grab her car keys off the hook and slam the front door behind me.

CHAPTER **14**

Adrenaline sizzles through my veins as I unlock Aunt Mindy's Camry, toss my bag in the back, and slide into the driver's seat. I haven't been behind the wheel in a while. Even though my hands are shaking, I manage to get the key into the ignition. I try to pull away from the curb, but there's a grinding noise and the car moves forward in slow jerks. I cuss at myself and release the parking brake.

Just as I'm starting to work up a little speed, a squirrel scampers into the street. I slam on the brakes. It freezes, tail rigid, and then dashes underneath a parked car. My heart thuds a million miles an hour as I hang a right off Aunt Mindy's street and onto the main road.

I'm not stealing her car, I tell myself. *I'm just borrowing it.* But I'm also driving without a license, so I scan the road for cops, and when a fire engine siren wails in the distance, I break out in a sweat.

I know I could still go back. I could park the car and hang Aunt Mindy's keys on the hook and she'd never suspect a thing. But some brave, wild part of me is in control, and I keep barreling toward the freeway, the late-afternoon sun in my eyes and a breeze from the cracked-open window tugging at my hair. *We live by our own rules,* I hear Mom say.

I've never driven in traffic before. The lane feels way too skinny, and I'm terrified I'll side-swipe one of the cars parked along the curb. When I swerve to avoid an SUV, the guy next to me honks and gives me the finger. I'd give it right back to him if I wasn't too chicken to take my hand off the wheel.

Without really deciding to, I merge onto I-5 South. I see a sign to Portland, and suddenly I know where I'm going. True, I don't know exactly where the rehab place is, but once I get to Portland, I'll ask around. There can't be that many of them.

I've never driven on the freeway before, either. I clench my jaw as I watch the speedometer needle climb to forty, then fifty, then sixty miles an hour. I'm still the slowest one on the road, so I push it to sixty-five. Tires hum on the asphalt.

That's when I see the cop in my rearview mirror.

He's one lane to the left of me. No lights or sirens—yet. I slow my speed to exactly sixty and grip the steering wheel so tight my fingers go white. A bead of sweat slides down the back of my neck and between my shoulder blades.

Now he's right behind me. I keep my eyes glued to the rearview mirror, and I've been holding my breath so long I feel like I'm going to pass out. I see the sign for the 45th Street NE exit up ahead and decide to go for it. If he's after me, I'm screwed anyway. I veer toward the exit, steeling myself for the flash of red and blue lights.

They never come. I glance out the side mirror to see the cop car sailing past the exit, just another drop in the rushing river of traffic.

As soon as I'm off the highway, I pull over, lay my head on the steering wheel, and suck in deep lungfuls of air. You couldn't pay me to get back on that freeway. I stare at a squished bug on the windshield, not knowing what to do. There's no way I can drive all the way to Oregon, but I can't go back to Aunt Mindy's either. I never want to see her stupid face again. I need some time to think, so I wind the car into the heart of the University District and park on a side street. Then I plug a few coins into the parking meter and head out on foot for University Way.

"The Ave," as everyone calls it, looks all college-student friendly, with purple and gold "Go, Huskies!" posters in the shop windows. But clusters of street kids hunker in front of those same stores, sucking on joints and trolling for spare change. When I pass an alleyway, I catch a whiff of pee.

I jam my hands in my pockets and walk with my head down. The smell of teriyaki and cheap tacos makes my stomach growl. It's got to be after four, and I haven't eaten since breakfast. I've got a few bucks in my pocket, but I'll need to save them for later, when I'll be really hungry.

"Hey," says a voice behind me.

I shoot a glance over my shoulder, scared it might be a cop.

"Hey, there." A girl about my age, dressed in baggy shorts and a stained T-shirt three sizes too big, breaks away from a group of kids camped out in front of Pagliacci Pizza and scrambles to catch up with me. She probably wants to hit me up for change, so I keep moving.

She comes up beside me. "Wait up, would you? I just want to talk to you. I saw you, and I said to myself, 'That girl could use a friend.'" She lays her hand on my arm. "You never have to be alone, you know. You've always got a friend in the Lord."

The kids behind her laugh and hoot. "That's right, baby. Spread the word," a guy with stringy black hair calls out.

If there's one thing I can't stand, it's someone trying to save me. Even if it's a load of crap. I step into the street, ignoring the honking of cars, and dodge my way across. I look back to make sure she hasn't followed and then duck into a little espresso bar. It's like walking into a time machine. Grateful Dead blasts from the stereo, and posters of wizards and serpents in Day-Glo colors plaster the black walls. The guy at the counter looks like a throwback too. His frazzly gray ponytail hangs between his shoulder blades, and a silver earring in the shape of a feather dangles from one ear.

"What'll it be, darlin'?" He pretends to juggle. "We've got your mocha and your cappuccino and your triple mochaccino and your supercalifragilistic any-way-you-want-it straight-up caffeine."

"Um," I say. I don't want to use up my money, but he seems so goofy and nice. I'll feel bad not ordering anything. "What's cheapest?"

"Lookin' for easy on the pocketbook, are you?" He holds one finger in the air, as if he's just had the world's most brilliant idea. "How about a nice tall glass of H_2O, on the house. You like ice?"

I take my glass of ice water to the little area in back. A shelf of old books lines one wall, and a couple of rocking chairs and a green-velvet couch that looks like something you'd see by the side of the road with a "Free" sign on it stand grouped in front of an empty fireplace. A huge furball of a black cat huddles on one end of the couch, aiming its pale green eyes at me.

"Hi, kitty," I say, and perch next to it.

The lady in a long black skirt who's sitting in one of the chairs looks up from her book. "That's Nostradamus."

I scratch his chin. His eyes narrow to slits and he starts to purr.

I've always wanted a cat. Most landlords won't let you have one, plus we move a lot. But even if we could, Mom says they're too much trouble. She says she doesn't want to be bothered with taking care of some animal all the time.

The long-skirt lady has gone back to her book and no one else is watching, so I ignore the couch's mildewy smell and curl up beside Nostradamus, cradling him in the crook of one elbow. Even though there's no fire, the room is warm, and the soft buzz of his purr makes me drowsy. I let myself close my eyes, just for a second.

Bad idea. When I wake up the counter guy is shaking my shoulder. "Sorry, darlin', I'm off in a few minutes."

I sit up and rake my fingers through my hair. Nostradamus is gone.

"Trust me, you don't want to be here when the manager gets in."

"Thanks," I mumble, and make my way out of the place still half-asleep.

Then I'm back on the street again, where the buildings throw long shadows on the sidewalk. My stomach is grumbling for real now. A guy who smells like moldy socks shakes a Styrofoam cup full of change at me as I pass and then cusses when I don't put anything in. The breeze has picked up, and I wish I hadn't left all my warm clothes in the car.

The car! I don't remember how much time I put on the meter, but for sure it wasn't enough. I sprint down the Ave and onto 50th. Even from a distance I can see the parking ticket fluttering beneath the windshield wiper. I swear under my breath.

The sun is hanging low on the horizon; soon it will be dark. Once I unlock the car, I root through my bag and throw on a flannel shirt. I had this idea I could park somewhere and sleep in the back seat, but now the thought of it gives me the creeps. I think about heading over to On the Wing to see if Valerie will let me spend the night, but I'm scared she might call Aunt Mindy.

Then I think of Tonya. We haven't talked since our fight, but I'm sure if I tell her what's going on, she'll be cool with letting me stay over. And I've spent the night with her a million times, so her dad wouldn't notice. If he's even in town.

When I pull up in front of her house, the sun is disappearing behind the trees. I hear voices and rap music inside, but it takes a minute for her to answer my knock. She opens the door a crack and pokes her head through.

"Stevie," she says, tugging at her tangle of dreads, "what are you doing here?"

I pretend not to notice how uncomfortable she looks. "Hey, Tonya."

We stare at each other for a couple of seconds, then she says, "So, what do you want?"

"Look, I'm sorry I acted like such a loser the other day. If you're not still mad at me, I was thinking we should hang out."

"Who's that?" a girl's voice calls from inside. Then Laura crowds in behind Tonya and gawks at me through her curtain of dyed-blond hair. "Oh, what a nice surprise. It's our little friend Stevie."

"Hi, Laura," I say. I'd love to whack the Maybelline right off her face, but under the circumstances that's not an option. "Hey, you guys want to watch a movie or something?"

Tonya glances at Laura and snaps her gum. "Um, we've already got plans."

I can feel any hope of food and a place to stay disappearing fast. "Well, I'm up for whatever."

Doug yells something in the background, and then Tonya says, "Okay, come on in." She opens the door wider and I step inside. Doug's slouched on the couch, and next to him is the Professor.

My heart does a double flip. "Hey," I say, "long time no see."

"Hey." His eyes meet mine for a second, then his attention goes back to fiddling with something on the coffee table.

Even though I can see what he's doing, I don't want to believe it. He's stuffing something into a glass pipe. Beside the pipe sits a lighter and a little plastic bag with chunks of whitish rock inside. It looks exactly like the stuff Mom sold to that guy at Drake's.

Tonya plops down next to the coffee table, pats the floor beside her, and smiles. "Don't worry. I've done it a couple of times, and it's no big deal."

I feel like I'm in the middle of a bad dream, the kind where you want to run but your legs won't move. At least she's smiling at me again. I drop onto the floor next to her.

The rapper on the stereo is talking a mile a minute. The Professor flicks the lighter and holds it under the bulb of the pipe. He moves the pipe in small circles and then puts the stem between his lips and inhales. When he breathes out again a sweet, burnt-plastic odor fills the air. I've smelled that odor before. On Mom.

It doesn't make sense. I always thought the Professor was so smart.

The Professor passes the pipe and lighter to Doug; Doug passes them to Laura. She takes a long hit.

Tonya's next. It takes her a couple of tries to get the lighter going. She inhales and then starts to cough.

"What a lightweight," Laura says.

Tonya laughs and pounds her chest, then hands the pipe to me.

It's light and smooth in my hand. I hate to admit it, but just breathing in the smell makes me feel close to Mom.

The Professor comes up behind me, his body warm against my back as he steadies my hand and holds the lighter under the pipe. "Now put the stem in your mouth."

They're all smiling, waiting for me to inhale. I could do it just this once and have a place to sleep tonight. I could be part of their world, of Mom's world. I hold the pipe to my lips and close my eyes.

"Go ahead, breathe in slow," the Professor says.

But before I can inhale, Drake's face floats in front of me.

He's running his hand across his buzzcut. I take the pipe out of my mouth.

"Are you going to take a hit or what?" Laura says.

Tonya gives her a little shove. "Chill, okay? She'll do it when she's ready." She smiles at me again. "Come on, it'll be fun."

I really want to make this work. I slide the pipe between my lips again, and I feel Mom right there with me. "Go ahead, baby," she's saying, and she's wrapping me up in her beautiful smile.

I'm so tired of fighting against it, of being the one who says no all the time. I'm ready to suck in the smoke that's dancing in the bulb when I think about the other Mom. The Mom who gets those calls from Drake and disappears for hours and then comes home talking nonstop and stays awake for days at a time. The Mom who finally falls asleep and then sleeps so long and hard, I can't wake her up. The Mom I'm scared to wake up even if I could because she'll bite my head off and tell me to get a friggin' life. I think about the times I wished she'd never wake up at all.

I hand the pipe to the Professor. "I can't do this."

Laura looks over at Tonya and rolls her eyes. "I told you."

I push myself off the floor and head for the front door.

The Professor's right behind me. "Hey, wait," he says, and touches my shoulder. "Don't leave."

I know I should keep going, but the sound of his voice and the weight of his hand draw me back. I turn, and his eyes are gazing into mine. His pupils are huge and dark.

"Nobody's forcing you to smoke." He puts his arm around my waist. "Let's go somewhere and talk, just you and me."

I have no place else to go, so I let him lead me down the hallway, past the bathroom. He pushes open the door at the end of the hall, and I shrink away.

"It's okay," he says in that same soft, easy voice. "Mike's out of town."

I hang back, but he just laughs. "It's not like we're going to break anything."

He pulls me into the room and shuts the door behind us. "There, now we can have a little privacy."

The room smells musty. In the few slivers of gray light that seep between the blinds, I can see Reba McEntire smiling down from the poster above the dresser.

The Professor sits on the edge of the bed.

Tonya's laughing over the music from the living room. They're still smoking out there, and all my instincts are telling me to get away. But when the Professor pats the bedspread, I sit down beside him.

"I've been thinking about you," he says.

I stare into the deep pools of his eyes, wishing I could believe him. But if he's thinking about me so much, how come he never calls?

"So you haven't smoked crystal before?"

"No. And I don't want to, either."

He starts twirling my hair with his fingers, the way he did in the car. "I like meth because it helps me focus. It makes me feel more alert and motivated."

His fingers move from my hair to the back of my neck. It feels like spiders crawling back there, and I have to force myself not to jerk away.

"A lot of people are scared of meth. But it's a member of the family of phenylethylamines—the same stuff you buy in the drugstore for nasal congestion."

So what if I can't pronounce the scientific name for it? He thinks he can impress me with all his big words, his alternate universes and black holes. He can fall into a black hole, for all I care. I'm seeing now it's all a bunch of crap, that I'm ten times smarter than he is. I shake his hand off me.

"What's the matter?" He lowers himself onto the bed and reaches for me. "I was kind of hoping we could finish what we started the other night."

After all the times I dreamed about that moment, I wouldn't kiss him now if you paid me. I push myself off the bed.

He sits up fast and grabs for me. "Hey, where you going?"

I don't bother to answer, just move toward the door.

"Don't get all pure and innocent on me," he calls. "You know you wanted to do it with Cole."

I slam the door behind me—hard.

CHAPTER 15

It's pitch dark now. I drive, not knowing or caring where I'm going. For a while I don't feel anything. Then, as I wander up and down the quiet side streets, my body starts to speak.

I'm starving, says my empty belly. Then an even louder voice says, *I need to pee!* I pull into a mini-mall and burst through the door of Westernco Donuts and into the restroom. I can hardly get my pants down fast enough.

Afterward I stay seated on the toilet and stare at the initials someone's scratched on the napkin disposal can. Finally I venture out and study myself in the mirror above the sink. Even though I feel like a different person than I did this morning, amazingly, on the outside, I still look like me.

After splashing some water on my face and wetting down my hair, I go out into the shop. The old lady with a hairnet standing behind the counter frowns at me and points to the sign that says, "Restrooms for Customers Only." The glare of the fluorescent lights makes the doughnuts lined up in the case look slick and greasy, but I hand her a dollar and ask for one of the glazed.

I'm gobbling down the doughnut at a little table by the window when a car pulls into the parking lot. It takes a few seconds to register the red and blue lights on top.

A hunk of glazed doughnut sticks in my throat. As the cop strides in the door, I bolt for the restroom. I lock myself in the last stall and sit on the toilet, hugging my knees to my chin. Any minute, I think, the restroom door will swing open and those heavy black cop shoes will come trudging toward me. But it doesn't happen.

I don't know how long I wait—half an hour, maybe longer. Long enough, I'm hoping, for the cop to finish a doughnut and a cup of coffee and leave. I creep out of the restroom, ready to duck back in if he's still there, but the only other person in the shop is a skinny old man sipping from a Styrofoam cup. I look out the window; the cop car is gone.

Such a surge of relief rushes through me that I give a big belly laugh. The lady with the hairnet purses her lips. I look her right in the eye and laugh again. Then I stroll out to the parking lot and start up the car.

I'm real good at driving forward down open country roads. Backing out of tight parking spots? Not so much. I inch slowly backward, then, just when I thought I've made it, *bam!* I smash Aunt Mindy's Camry into a light pole.

The relief I felt a minute ago smashes right along with it. I sit for a couple of minutes with my face in my hands. Finally I get up the nerve to get out and check the damage. There's a big, honking crack in the bumper, and one of the taillights is shattered.

At least the car still drives. There's nowhere else to go, so I hang a left and wind through Crown Hill, back to the old apartment building, which is lit by a full moon and the eerie glow of streetlights. I never really noticed before how tacky it looks, the way all the units are painted a pukey greenish color and most people have sheets strung up in their windows instead of curtains. The poop-covered Toyota still sits in Mom's parking space. There's a light on in my room; I wish it was me curled up in bed there tonight.

I park the car and hoist myself onto the low wall in front of the complex. I can feel the cold even through my flannel shirt, but I don't care anymore. I think about all the good times we had in that apartment: snuggling up and watching late-night TV, ordering pizzas, playing poker at the kitchen table, telling stories and laughing so hard we could barely breathe. There were some bad times too: Mom cussing out the landlord when he came to collect our rent, the night I had to stay with the neighbors because Mom got beat up. Still, even with all the bad, I'd give a million bucks to be living my old life right now.

I lean my head back and check out the stars. Sometimes they look so close I feel like I could touch them, but tonight they seem light-years away. I think about how alone I am, floating out here in this endless universe. I'm aching for someone to talk to. Not the Professor—I'm done with him. Not Tonya either.

Alan. I wish he was here right now. We'd kick back and shoot the breeze, talk about birds, talk about nothing. Or maybe we'd just sit and not talk, or—

A car honks. I tense, figuring it's some jerk trying to pick me up. Then I hear Aunt Mindy's voice.

"Stevie, is that you?"

I squint into the dark and realize with a jolt that it's Rick's Maserati idling by the curb. You-Know-Who is calling to me through his passenger side window.

"Come on. You can't sit there all night."

Wanna bet? I say with my eyes.

She gets out of the car and slams the door. Then she leans in through the window and says something to Rick. He takes off, and she marches over to her Camry. I'm scared she'll notice the crack in the bumper, but she climbs in and opens the passenger door. "Get in!" she shouts.

I think about making a run for it, but I know it's no use. I have nowhere else to go. I drop off the wall and get in the car.

At first we don't say anything. I don't even look at her. When she finally breaks the silence, her voice is shaking. "I am so angry with you." Her face looks hard and tight, and she's holding onto her thighs like she's scared she might hit me. "What were you thinking, Stevie? You don't know how to drive a car."

"I've driven one before, okay?"

"No, not okay. For your information, it's against the law to drive without a license."

"Fine. Just take me to jail, then."

"You don't know how close I came to calling the police. I told Rick, 'Let's go by the apartment one more time.' If we didn't find you here . . . My God, Stevie, don't you realize you could have been killed?"

"Like you care," I say under my breath.

"What did you say?" She spits out each word.

"Like you care." I can spit words too.

She grabs me by both shoulders. "If I didn't care, do you think I would have called everyone I know, anyone who might have seen you? Do you think I would have forced Rick to drive every square inch of this city looking for you? You have no idea what you put me through. Here I'm thinking we're going to find you on a highway somewhere with your head through the windshield." She puts her hands over her face and starts to sob.

I don't know what to do, so I just sit there and watch her.

After a minute or so she wipes her eyes on her sleeve. "Look, are you hungry?"

I don't answer.

"Well, I am. Let's grab a burger at Dick's."

I wonder if she's gone nuts. I've never seen her eat a burger—she lives on salad and fish and energy bars. But sure enough, she makes me hand over the keys and then drives us the two blocks to Dick's. She slips me a twenty and says, "Get me a cheeseburger with extra onions, and some fries. And something for yourself, if you want."

I go to the walk-up window and order Aunt Mindy's stuff and a double Deluxe, onion rings, and a vanilla shake for me. The burgers smell so good and I'm so hungry, I start to dig in as soon as I get in the car.

"Hang on. We're not eating in a parking lot." She pulls onto Holman and follows it as it turns into 15th, then takes a right on 75th and parks by the Overlook, this little park with a chain-link fence along one side.

"I'll take that cheeseburger now," she says.

I hand her the warm burger, then unwrap my own and take a huge bite. Mayonnaise dribbles down my chin.

We chew on our food in silence for a minute. Then she turns to me and I brace myself for another lecture, but she just says, "Promise you won't ever scare me like that again."

"Whatever," I mumble around a mouthful of burger.

"Come on, let's look at the view." She wipes her hands on a napkin, stuffs her keys into her pocket, and strolls toward the fence.

I sit in the car sipping my shake, my shoulders hunched up to my ears. Aunt Mindy motions me over, but I ignore her. She puts her hands on her hips and gives me the get-your-butt-over-here stare.

Once I'm standing beside her, she says, "Tell me this isn't gorgeous."

I'm not usually big on views, but this one's not half bad. On the other side of the chain-link fence, with moonlight shining on their sails, the boats in Shilshole Bay Marina look like ghosts floating on the water. Beyond them, Puget Sound stretches toward the Olympics. It's quiet except for the lonely bark of a seal in the distance.

"I can understand why you're angry," she says. "We have a hard time seeing eye to eye when it comes to your mom."

I tense up, thinking we're headed for another fight.

"And I really should have told you about Rick."

Yeah, that.

"It was the last thing I was expecting. A few weeks ago he called and asked if we could get together and talk about how you were doing. We had coffee, and coffee led to dinner and—"

"Okay, okay, I get the picture."

"We've been spending some time together, and, well, we really should have told you sooner. We just wanted to see where it was going before we said anything." She turns to me. The moonlight makes her face look smooth and glowing, like the ladies on those skin-cream commercials. For the first time I sort of get what Rick might see in her. "It's been a long time since I've felt this way about someone. I hope you won't let this come between us, Stevie."

I'm trying my best to stay mad at her, but it's not working. I sigh and say, "Fine."

The seal barks again, but this time it doesn't sound so lonely. We stare out over the water for a minute more.

I clear my throat. "I guess I should tell you. I got a parking ticket."

"Not a big deal. You can pay for it with your allowance."

"And I backed into a pole. There's a big crack in the bumper and one of the taillights is smashed."

She blows air through her lips. "That's a bigger deal, but we'll work it out. Anything else you need to tell me?"

I think about the sweet, burnt-plastic smell and the Professor's crystal-dark pupils staring into mine. Some things I just can't tell Aunt Mindy.

She glances at me, then back at the water. "I guess there's something I need to tell you too. Your mom called again. She's still thinking about leaving rehab. Apparently some friend of hers is willing to loan her the money for bus fare. But if you encouraged her to finish out her twelve weeks, maybe she'd do it."

"I want her to come home!"

Her voice softens. "I know you do. But June has a chance to kick this thing. She might think she's okay now, but wait until she's back in the city again. There's going to be a lot of temptation."

I know she's right, but my heart keeps shouting that I want Mom back.

"I understand that you have a hard time believing this, but I really do want the best for your mom. She hasn't always made great choices, but she's my sister, and I love her." She puts her hand on my arm for a second, then pulls it away. "Just like I love you."

The breeze is starting to pick up, so I hug my shirt close.

"You're cold. Let's get out of here."

We drive without saying anything, but it's a different kind of silence than before. It's a window instead of a wall.

We pull up in front of the house. Before she turns off the ignition, she says, "I want you to give this some serious thought. Sleep on it, and if it feels right, we'll call your mom in the morning."

I'm so wiped out I could die, but I can't fall asleep. I go over things every which way as I watch the clock turn over to two, then three, then four in the morning. I make lists in my head. One is "Reasons Mom Should Stay in Rehab." It's got lots of important things on it, like *She'll get better for sure* and *She won't start using crystal again.* The other list, "Reasons Mom Should Come Home," only has one thing on it: *Because I want her to.*

By five in the morning, I'm exhausted but I'm sure. When I finally fall asleep, I have that dream again. The blue-flowered blanket surrounds me from toe to chin, and Mom's breath as she leans in to kiss me is warm on my cheek. "Don't worry, Stevie," she whispers in that husky voice of hers. "I'll take care of you."

At nine Aunt Mindy makes the call. Once she gets Mom on the line, she hands the phone to me. "Good luck," she whispers, then leaves me alone.

"Mom? Are you there?"

She wraps me up in her big, warm laugh. "How you doing, baby? My God, it's good to hear your voice."

I'm so choked up I can hardly talk. "Good to hear yours too."

"So, you ready to see your old mom again?"

Yes, yes, yes! I want to tell her, but I know I have to be strong. "Yes, but . . ." I swallow. "But I think you should finish your program."

There's a long silence on the other end. "You don't want me to come home?"

"I didn't say that. I just want you to—"

"I can't believe it. My own daughter doesn't want me to come home."

"That's not what I'm saying!"

"This is exactly what I was afraid would happen." She sighs. When she speaks again her voice is heavy. "You've changed, baby. I feel like I don't know you anymore."

The world starts to crumble around me. The walls slide toward the floor, and the phone turns to dust in my hands.

"I think Mindy's been playing mind games with you. That's what's going on, isn't it? She's got you all mixed up so you don't know what you want."

"Mom . . ." I'm so confused I start to sob.

"Aww, baby, don't cry. See, you do want me to come back, don't you, honey pie?"

Honey pie. The second she says those words, everything on my Reasons-Mom-Should-Stay-in-Rehab list disappears.

"Yes," I say. "I want you to come home. Now."

CHAPTER 16

For the next two days, I feel like I'm in the middle of a windstorm. One minute I'm laughing and dancing and yelling "Mom's coming home on Saturday!" loud enough for everyone in the world to hear. Then, *whoosh!* A big gust of wind comes by and yanks me in the other direction, and I'm so disgusted at myself for being selfish I want to crawl in a hole and disappear. *Whoosh!* I get jerked one way. *Whoosh!* Back the other way. And when Aunt Mindy purses her lips and says, "Leave it to June to get exactly what she wants," I feel like I'm being blown apart and smashed to the ground.

But finally it's Saturday. The weather has warmed up again, and by noon it's so hot my T-shirt sticks to my back. Mom's bus doesn't get in until 4:48, but I'm already stressing. What do you wear to celebrate your mom coming home from rehab?

I think about wearing the outfit Aunt Mindy bought me, but I know Mom would hate it, so I slip into my old plaid boxers and Hello Kitty tank. Then I catch sight of myself in the mirror. I look like a complete dork. I try on everything I own, but nothing looks right.

Half an hour and twenty outfits later, I decide to go ahead and wear my new gray pants. I pull on the top and adjust the cutout so it hits my collarbone just right. When Mom looks at me, I don't want her to see the same scared kid she left two months ago. I want her to see the Stevie I am now, the one Valerie trusts with the birds, the one who's good at drawings and numbers. I want her to see the Stevie who could actually be somebody.

•—◆—•

I push my way through the crowded bus station to the waiting area in back. Aunt Mindy's inside at the Starbucks stand, but I want to see Mom the second she gets in.

It finally pulls up, twenty-five minutes late. One by one the passengers straggle off: a tall black lady with a red suitcase, a couple of pimple-faced guys plugged into iPods, a bleary-eyed mom with a baby in one arm and a folded-up stroller in the other.

Then the most beautiful woman I've ever seen steps off the bus. She's wearing tight, faded jeans, and a little pot belly peeks out under a black tank that shouts "Ozzy Rules!" across her chest in big silver letters. Her dark hair billows around her head, and her red-lipsticked smile carves a dimple in her left cheek, daring you not to notice her. Her cheeks have filled out since I saw her in Drake's window, but there are new wrinkles across her forehead and at the corners of her eyes.

I see her spot me and all the sounds and smells of the bus station fade away. I rush to her.

"Mom!"

She sets down her bag and grabs me up in a bear hug. "Hey, honey pie." Her jasmine-and-cigarette smell is exactly like I remembered it.

We hang on for a minute, then gradually the world returns—the smells of coffee and sweat, the sound of ringing cell phones. Mom lets go and steps back.

Just then Aunt Mindy comes strolling toward us. "June," she says with a tight smile, "welcome back."

Mom takes one look at the Starbucks cup in Aunt Mindy's hand. "Regular coffee still not good enough for you, huh?" Then she looks me up and down. "And I see you've been playing Dress the Dolly."

I could kick myself for not sticking with the boxers.

Nobody says a word on the way home. When Mom cracks open the window and lights up a cigarette, Aunt Mindy grips the steering wheel but doesn't tell her to put it out. Even though I'm dying to ask Mom a million questions about rehab, I know she won't tell me anything right now.

Later that evening Aunt Mindy tosses a blanket and pillow onto the couch and says, "I'll let the two of you wrangle over who gets the guest room." Then she heads off to her bedroom and shuts the door.

"I can sleep out here," I tell Mom, then I go change into flannel bottoms and a tank.

But when I come back, she says she's fine with the couch. She slips off her jeans and crawls under the blanket. She tells me to turn out the light, and then, just like I'm hoping she will, she motions for me to join her. I prop myself against the other end of the couch so I can see her face. Our legs twine together underneath the blanket.

She smiles at me and shakes her head. Even in the dim light from the hallway, I can see the sharp outline of her silhouette. "Kind of like old times, isn't it, baby?"

I wiggle my toes against her. I wish I could stay like this forever, feeling the warmth of her legs against mine.

"And you know those plans we were always making? Well, they're starting to come together. I've been talking to this guy about my jewelry business, and he's real excited about it. Wants to set me up with a website and everything."

"Nice. Did you meet him at the rehab place?"

She grunts. "You kidding? One of those losers? No, this was a guy I ran into on the bus."

I get a sinking feeling. "But you must have met some cool people there."

She reaches down and squeezes my calf. "Come on, baby, that's in the past. You know me. I'm all about the future."

When Mom starts to doze off a while later, I slip out from under the blankets and pad down the hallway to the guest room, where I fall into a restless sleep. Tired as I am, I keep bolting awake with my heart pounding. Three times during the night, I tiptoe out to the living room to make sure Mom is still there.

The fourth time I wake up to check, it's almost six in the morning. Birds have started singing outside the windows, and weak light filters in through the blinds. The heat hasn't cranked up yet, so I throw on my robe.

Mom's still asleep, her dark curls splayed across the pillow. She must have gotten cold, because she's got an extra blanket thrown across her legs. When I move closer I see it's the blue-flowered blanket from my memory. As I cinch my robe at the waist and watch the gentle rise and fall of Mom's chest, I think back to the time long ago when we lived with Aunt Mindy in that little place in Helena, Montana. I remember peeking into the closet and seeing the blanket all folded up. I thought it was so pretty, and I always asked Mom if I could take it out, but she never let me.

Then one day she did take it out of the closet, and she wrapped it around me. I know she did. But the memory is so dim I've always wondered if I made the whole thing up. Seeing Mom asleep under the blanket now, knowing she must have dragged it all the way to rehab and back, I decide I'm finally sure it really happened.

Just like she did to me so long ago, I lean over and kiss her cheek. "Don't worry, Mom," I whisper. "I'll take care of you."

• ◆ •

Aunt Mindy says we can stay at her place a week or two until Mom gets back on her feet, but after a couple of days I can tell Mom's getting antsy. Aunt Mindy won't let her smoke in the house, so she spends most of her time out on the back deck, even when it rains, smoking and staring into space.

"Did they let you smoke in rehab?" I ask her late one afternoon, when streaks of pink color the gray sky and light up the jagged ridges of the Cascades. I keep asking about rehab, but she still hasn't told me much.

She takes a drag off her cigarette and waves the smoke away with one hand. "If they tried to take my cigs away, I'd a been out of there in ten seconds flat."

I plop down in the white plastic patio chair next to hers and let my eyes wander over her face, memorizing every line, every shadow.

"What was it like there?"

She shrugs. "You seen one prison, you seen them all."

"But Aunt Mindy said—"

She reaches over and pats my cheek. "Let it go, baby. I'm back, okay?" She stubs out her cigarette. "It's freezing out here. Let's go in and order up a pizza." She winks at me. "Mindy's buying; we might as well make it a large."

On Saturday night Aunt Mindy invites Rick over for dinner. She says he's important in my life and that Mom should meet him, but I can't help wondering if she just wants to show him off and rub Mom's face in it.

He's set to come over at seven. Mom sits outside and smokes while I polish the silverware and Aunt Mindy cooks. Every time

Aunt Mindy turns her back, I stuff my face with potato chips to quiet the jumpiness in my belly. When Mom comes in, winks at me, and says, "Guess I'd better slip into something uncomfortable," I nearly finish off the bag.

As soon as she struts out of the bedroom, I know there's going to be trouble. She's got on a top so low-cut you can see the head of the mermaid tattooed on her left boob. A pair of the beaded earrings she makes dangle from each ear, and I can smell her jasmine perfume a mile away. But what scares me most are her bare feet—"the sexiest part of a woman's body is her feet," she likes to say—and the look on her face when I let Rick in the front door. He's wearing white pants and a black shirt that shows off his muscles.

"Mom, this is my tutor, Rick."

She holds out her hand and turns on the knock-your-socks-off smile that shows off the dimple in her left cheek, the smile she saves for her customers with money. "June," she says.

He takes hold of her fingertips, and for a second I think he's about to kiss her hand, but then he gives it a gentle shake. "Melinda's told me a lot about you."

Mom's smile sours a bit. "Only nice things, I bet." She turns and calls into the kitchen. "Mindy, your boyfriend's here."

Aunt Mindy rushes into the living room wearing an oven mitt. Her face is pink, and a wispy curl sticks to her forehead. "Hi, Rick. I'm almost done in there. Make yourself at home." She takes one look at Mom and turns even pinker. "June, could you help me for a minute?"

"But I'm entertaining our guest."

"June . . ."

"All right, already, I'm coming." She stalks after Aunt Mindy.

Rick clears his throat. "You must be happy your mom is back."

"Yeah," I say, but I'm straining to hear what's going on in the kitchen. Finally the two of them come out, Mom carrying glasses and cradling a bottle of wine under her arm and Aunt Mindy balancing a platter of veggies and dip on one hand. They're both scowling.

Rick jumps to his feet. "Here, let me help you with that." He takes the tray from Aunt Mindy, sets it on the coffee table, and gives her a peck on the cheek.

"Who wants wine?" Mom asks. She sets the glasses down next to the veggie tray. "I know I could use some." She fills one of the glasses and takes a big swallow. Then she shoots Aunt Mindy a dirty look, fills a second wineglass, and holds it out to her. "Bet you could use a drink, too." Aunt Mindy snatches the glass and heads back into the kitchen.

Next Mom turns to Rick, who's gone back to his seat on the couch, and gives him that smile again. "And I know you're going to need one." She keeps her eyes locked on his while she fills the glass. When she hands it to him, she leans over so far that I can see the mermaid's tail from where I'm standing. If I were that mermaid, I'd swim the hell out of here.

Then she pours a fourth glass of wine and hands it to me. "And one for you, baby."

Aunt Mindy comes out of the kitchen, spots my glass, and plants her hands on her hips. "What do you think you're doing?"

"I think she's old enough to have a little wine."

"She's only fifteen, June."

"You think I don't know how old my own daughter is?" She nods at me. "Go ahead and drink it, honey pie."

Rick gets up and nabs the glass from me. "I have to agree with Melinda. Stevie is underage."

That shuts Mom up for a few minutes, but then it's the same thing all through dinner. Mom snags the seat right next to Rick and keeps leaning in and showing off her mermaid while Aunt Mindy fumes at the head of the table. I'm scared to peek underneath. Mom's probably trying to play footsie with him, too.

Finally we make it to dessert. It's Aunt Mindy's chocolate mousse, which is heaven on a spoon. Rick tastes it, closes his eyes, and says, "Melinda, you've outdone yourself."

Mom licks her spoon and says, "Mmm. Better than sex." Then she winks at Rick. "Well, almost."

I set down my spoon. Maybe it's those chips I ate earlier, but I'm not really hungry anymore.

Aunt Mindy pushes her chair away from the table. "Okay, June, that's it. I'm not going to sit here and be made a fool of."

"Oh, come on. I'm just trying to lighten things up."

"You can go spread your sunshine somewhere else. I want you out of here by tomorrow morning."

Rick glances at me. "Melinda, let's give it some—"

"If anyone wants me, I'll be in my room," she says, and then heads down the hallway.

Rick puts his hand on my arm. "Let me talk to her." Then he goes after her.

That leaves me and Mom at the table. She scoops up another spoonful of mousse. "This stuff is to die for. And so is your tutor, by the way."

"I told you, he's going out with Aunt Mindy."

"That won't last." She laughs and cups her hands under her boobs. "He needs a woman who's got a little meat on her."

"Mom, don't. They're happy."

The second it's out of my mouth, I wish I could take it back.

Mom slams down her spoon. "Well, isn't that nice. Of course we want Mindy to be happy. She's skinny, she's swimming in dough, but that's not enough. Oh, no. We've got to make sure she's happy, too."

"She's not 'swimming in dough,' Mom. And she works really hard."

"Oh, so now you're defending her?"

"No, I just—"

"She's always been on my case to hand you over; well, maybe I should. Maybe I should let you stay here so she can jump for friggin' joy."

"I don't want to stay here."

She pushes her chair away from the table and stands. "She thinks she's doing me a big favor, letting me sleep on her precious couch. Well, I've got other places I can stay." She heads for the living room. "You want to stay here and play Happy Family with Mindy, fine."

I run after her and throw my arms around her waist. "I want to be with you!"

I feel her hand in my hair. "Hush, baby. Calm down. You really want to come with me, huh?"

"Yes." Maybe if I can get her out of here, away from Aunt Mindy, things will be better.

"And you won't go talking to Mindy behind my back again?"

"No. I promise."

She peels my arms from around her waist. "Go to bed, then. I got to make a few calls. We'll talk in the morning."

I lie awake half the night, listening to Mom and Aunt Mindy argue in the living room. Finally I pull the pillow over my head, close my eyes, and try to find the dream about the blue-flowered blanket. But tonight the dream won't come.

CHAPTER 17

In the morning Mom tells me we're moving out. Her friend Tina has an extra room in the basement, and I can sleep in her living room. I'm already packed, so I sit on the bed and wait while Mom takes a shower.

Sun streams through the window, blazing a rectangle onto the bedspread. I set my hand in the rectangle and let it lie there, like a lizard on a rock, soaking up the warmth. I stare out at the view of the mountains and breathe in the vanilla scent of the candle by the bed.

There's a knock at the door; Aunt Mindy pokes her head in. "Can I come in for a second?"

"I guess."

She sits beside me on the bed. "How are you feeling this morning?"

I shrug.

"I'm sorry about all that business last night. I hope you know it had nothing to do with you." She takes my hand, the one warm from the sun. "You don't have to leave, you know. You're more than welcome to stay with me."

"I want to be with Mom."

She looks at me for a long time. Then she looks away. "I understand. But I want you to know I'm here, anytime you need me." She puts her arms around me, and I have to bite my lip to keep from bawling. I don't know what's wrong with me; I've been waiting all summer for the chance to get away from her.

Then Mom calls from the bathroom: "I'll be ready in five minutes. You got some change for the bus?"

Aunt Mindy presses something into my hand. "Just in case," she says. Then her face crinkles up, and she rushes out of the room.

I open my hand and see a hundred-dollar bill.

Tina's house is on a side street, right off Aurora and Northgate Way, not too far from where I found the crow. She's got two other roommates: Dave, a skinny guy with a straggly blond ponytail, and a fat chick named Cory. Tina's not fat or skinny, but her skin is dark with light patches on it, like a tan that's peeling off.

I'm not used to living with so many people. There are sounds all the time: doors opening and closing, pots and pans clanging, toilets flushing. There are strange smells too. Dave is always making stir-fry with broccoli and garlic, and Cory stinks up the bathroom. Plus the house isn't that clean. Cobwebs cling to the ceiling, ants roam the kitchen counter, and a huge spider has set up shop in one corner of the shower. I'm hoping Mom's still got those business deals cooking, because it feels like our NTD House is fading into the *far*-distant future.

I sleep on a futon on the living room floor. People wander in and out, which means I have to keep my stuff with Mom's in the basement and change down there. The only safe place to stow my heart-shaped box, with the hundred-dollar bill inside, is under Mom's bed.

I stick to Mom like the spider to its web. I'd even follow her into the bathroom if she'd let me. Sometimes she gets ticked and says, "Give me a little space, would you?" I was kind of hoping she'd find another place to work, but she seems happy to get back to her job at the nightclub. Tina works there too, so most nights they take off together in Tina's rusty Dodge Dart.

Me, I don't go anywhere. When Mom's awake I'm with her, when she's at the club I hang out on the futon and work on my drawings. I still jump if the phone rings and count the hours every time she leaves the house. She makes me promise again to stay away from Aunt Mindy, says we don't need her screwing things up just when we're getting them back together. Rick offers to come to the house to tutor me, but I can't stand the thought of him smelling Dave's stir-fry or seeing Cory's Tampax wrappers in the bathroom waste-basket. And even though I miss working at On the Wing, I call Valerie and tell her I need to take a break. Right now being with Mom is the only thing that matters.

One afternoon about three weeks after we move in, I let down my guard. It's near the end of July, and fall's on the way: The leaves are turning yellow, and people on the street stroll by in jeans and sweatshirts instead of shorts. Mom's asleep in the basement, and I figure it won't hurt if I go out, just for a little while.

My plan is to grab myself a Coke at the convenience store on Aurora and then head right back. The breeze has a bite to it, so I walk fast, keeping my eyes on the ground.

The *beep, beep, beep* of the bus across the street lowering its wheelchair ramp makes me look up. Pictures of kids in knit sweaters, lugging stacks of books, smile at me from the side of the bus. *Macy's Back to School Blowout,* the giant ad says.

I hug myself tight; goose bumps cover my arms. I've hardly thought about school at all since I left Aunt Mindy's. Mom hasn't asked me about it either. In fact, now that I think of it, she hasn't asked me about anything.

Aunt Mindy was always full of questions: When are you going to talk to your counselor again? What are your plans for next year? What about college? I picture her in her purple workout gear, leaning against the kitchen counter with that intense look she gets, telling me I need to start thinking about the future before it leaves me behind.

A hole opens up inside me that only seeing Aunt Mindy can fill. I hate to admit it, but I miss the smell of her coffee, her stupid notes. I even miss her nagging. So when the number 75 bus rumbles past, I scrap my plan to get a Coke and race to catch it. I've never taken it before, but I'm pretty sure it goes through Wedgewood.

"Wait up!" I yell. I wave my arms, but the driver doesn't see me. I make it to the bus stop, pissed and out of breath, just as he's pulling away.

I've made up my mind to head back to Tina's when a silver Honda that looks just like Valerie's drives up next to me.

"Need a ride?"

The second I hear Alan's voice, my heart goes into overdrive. It's been at least a month since the day I ran away from him, and I was sure he'd written me off by now. I haven't written him off, though. Actually, he's been on my mind a lot lately. I wonder if he keeps going over that day in the aviary the way I do.

"You want a lift or what?" he says.

"Sure." I tug open the passenger door and climb in.

"So, where you headed?" Alan asks.

"My aunt's house. In Wedgewood, right off Seventy-fifth."

"I'm doing a few errands for Valerie, but they're no big deal. I can run you over there."

He pulls into traffic, and we don't say anything for a few

minutes. While he drives, I study his profile. It's weird how all the things I used to hate about him—the way his dark hair falls into his eyes, his army jacket, even his stupid sunglasses—are making my insides go into serious meltdown.

"Sorry I haven't been around in a while," I say.

He hangs a left on 80th. "Yeah, what's up with that?"

"Well, for one thing, my mom came back."

"Cool." He reaches for the dashboard like he's about to turn on the radio. If I don't say it now, I never will.

"But I guess the main thing is, I was nervous about seeing you again."

He puts his hand back on the wheel and stares straight ahead.

"Well, aren't you going to say anything?" I ask.

"What do you want me to say? You're the one that took off."

"I can explain—"

"You don't have to explain anything. I got the message loud and clear."

His voice has that clamped-down sound that makes me want to get out of the car and forget the whole thing. But I'm not going to do that. Not this time.

"No, you don't get it. I didn't take off because of you. There was this other guy, sort of, and I wasn't sure . . . But that's over now."

"Whatever."

I can't really think of anything else to say. He turns on the radio, and we listen to the DJ on 107.7 yammer about the summer concert we can't afford to miss.

"Make a left here," I say when we get to Aunt Mindy's street.

I can tell right off she's not home—the blinds are closed, and her car's not in the driveway—but I get out anyway.

"Thanks," I say. "See you around."

He drives off without a word.

I stand on Aunt Mindy's front porch, trying to peek through the blinds. I was looking forward to telling her about Tina and Cory and Dave and maybe having her make me a cup of coffee, nice and strong. I knock just in case, but of course there's no answer. I could use my key, but what's the point of going in? I tell myself I'm being stupid, that if I spent more than five minutes with her I'd go nuts. But when I see Mom's plant standing full and leafy in her flowerbed, the clusters of blue flowers just starting to fade from the autumn chill, I have to fight away the tears.

When the bus gets me home forty-five minutes later, Mom's not in her bedroom. She's not in the bathroom, either. Dave's in the kitchen chopping garlic, but when I ask him if he's seen her, he shakes his head. I could kick myself for being out so long.

She probably walked down to the store for cigarettes, or maybe she went to McDonald's for a burger. I spread my drawing stuff out on the living room floor and take deep breaths to calm myself, but I can't concentrate. It's like the ants from the kitchen are crawling all over my legs, making me run to the window every few minutes.

Finally I give up trying to work on my drawing. I count the seconds in my head to make them go by faster; every one seems a million years long. I stare at the door as if wishing hard enough could make Mom walk through it. That's when I notice the blinking red light on Tina's caller ID.

I tell myself it's probably for Tina or Dave. But of course I have to look. I push the little button and the name comes up, the one I've been dreading: *Uttley, Drake.*

I grab the caller ID box and slam it against the wall with a loud *crack*. Chips of paint fall to the floor, leaving a ragged scar. I try to stick the paint chips back onto the wall, but they fall off again. *Nice, Stevie. Tina gives us a place to stay, and you go and wreck her stuff.*

When Mom finally strolls through the door twenty minutes later, I rush to meet her. "Where were you?"

"I went to get some cigs." She takes one look at my face. "Jesus, baby, what's eating you?"

"I've been waiting half an hour. It doesn't take that long to get cigarettes." Of course I know she's been gone longer than that, but I'm not about to bring up the time I spent getting to and from Aunt Mindy's.

She looks at me like I've gone insane. "It's a nice day. I went for a walk. Is there a problem?"

"He called you, didn't he?"

"Who called me?" She glances at the phone, then her gaze travels to the dent in the wall. "What happened here?"

"Drake. You can't lie to me. I saw his name on the caller ID."

She gets close to the dent and runs her finger across it. Then she picks up the busted caller ID and shoves it in my face. "I hope you've got the money to pay for this, 'cause I sure as hell don't."

"Why won't you answer me?"

She holds up her hands. "Okay, okay. You want to know what happened? Drake heard I was in town, so he called me. He asked if I wanted to meet for a beer. I said no, I was done with him and his crap."

I search her face, trying to figure out if she's telling the truth.

"Then I went to the store to buy myself a pack of cigarettes. End of story. You satisfied?"

My legs feel so weak, I have to lean against the wall. "Sorry. It's just—"

"I know, honey pie. Believe me, I know. But you got to trust me this time. Give me a chance to show you I've changed."

I can't stop the tears that are welling in my eyes. I'm the one who can't be trusted, running off to Aunt Mindy's like that.

"Of course I trust you," I say.

She puts her arms around me, and the world feels whole again.

Then she laughs and gives me a little shake. "Get yourself a life, would you?"

She smiles at me to let me know she's joking.

I smile back.

Mom's right: I can't keep hanging around, watching over her every second. Besides, my world feels like it's shrinking; the water-stained walls of Tina's house are all I ever see. And even though it's great to be with Mom, I keep going back in my mind to the day Alan kissed me in the aviary. Okay, the day we kissed each other. The more I think about it, the more I know I can't leave things weird and unfinished between us. The more I think about it, the more I know I want to kiss him again.

The next afternoon, once Mom goes to bed, I squeeze myself into a pair of jeans, throw on a shirt and a fringed vest, and bus over to On the Wing. I take a deep breath, then let myself in the cage-room door.

The rustle of wings greets me. I wander from cage to cage, peeking to see who's inside. I look around for the crow with the broken wing but don't see it anywhere. It must have graduated to the aviary by now.

Thinking Alan might be in the other part of the house, I tiptoe through the kitchen, into the living room. I can smell Valerie's perfume, and Alan's jacket hangs on the back of a chair, but no one seems to be around.

Then I hear running water in the bathroom, and over that the sound of someone singing the *Sesame Street* theme song. The voice is high and squeaky, but there's no doubt in my mind it's Alan's. I just about lose it. Alan Parker, Mr. I'm-Too-Cool-to-Crack-a-Smile, is singing in the shower.

I creep right up to the bathroom door and listen. Once he finishes the *Sesame Street* song, he moves on to opera. "Fee-ga-ro. Feegaro feegaro feegaro feegaro FEE-ga-ro," he belts in a booming voice.

I have to bite my lip to keep from laughing out loud. One thing you can say about Alan, at least he's never boring. When he turns off the water, I hurry to the backyard so he won't know I was listening.

As soon as I get near to the aviaries, the birds inside start to chirp and caw. "Feegaro, feegaro," I sing back at them. I spend a few minutes at the first aviary, checking out some new sparrows and a baby jay.

Then I draw close to the wire mesh of the second aviary and peer inside. A robin perches on a branch near the roof. Its feathers are gray and its chest is covered with dark spots. It gives a shrill chirp, then swoops toward the food dish on the ground. It's Tweety Bird. I watch as she lifts her yellow beak to ease an earthworm down her throat. I used to hate it that she didn't need me anymore; now I feel proud.

"Hi, Tweety."

"Still calling it by a cute little name, I see."

I whip around, and there's Alan, standing behind me with a feeding tray. Sunglasses hide his eyes, and his wet hair lies slick against his head. I imagine him shampooing it and singing away. I have to choke back a laugh.

"Where'd you come from?" I say, trying to look surprised. "You scared the heck out of me."

It's true; my heart is pounding, but not because I'm scared. His T-shirt hugs his chest, and his face looks so smooth and clean it's all I can do not to reach out and touch it.

He sets the tray on the ground. "I wasn't exactly expecting you to show up, either."

Tweety Bird flits from the food dish back to her branch.

"We're going to release that robin soon," he says. "Couple of weeks, probably. Give it a chance to find a flock before the weather starts getting cold."

"Want me to help feed?" I ask.

He grabs the water pitcher and hands me the container of dry food. We let ourselves into the first aviary and refill the dishes. For a minute it's quiet except for the sound of birds swooping down to eat.

"There is no other guy, is there?" he finally asks.

"What are you talking about?"

"That day in the car. You said you took off because of some other guy, but I think you lied. I think you took off because I'm a complete loser, and because of how I treated you."

I kneel and pretend to watch the birds peck at the food. Something tells me I'll be better off not saying anything.

"I can't help it sometimes. I just get out of control and end up saying stupid stuff, even when I don't mean it."

I think about some of the lousy things I've said to Aunt Mindy. "Hey, you're not the only one."

"No, I'm serious. Whenever things start going halfway decent, I screw them up. Since they're going to dump me anyway, I figure I might as well give them a reason."

I stand and brush off my jeans. "Wait a second; you lost me. Who's 'they'?"

He gives a sarcastic laugh. "My loving foster families. I've been in eight homes since I was six, and kicked out of every one."

I remember the adoption lady saying he'd moved around a lot, but I can't even imagine living with eight different families. "What happened to your mom and dad?"

"Apparently Mom had a drinking problem. Not that I remember or anything. I never met my dad. The only one who's still around is my caseworker, and I'm surprised she hasn't given up on me. Everybody else does."

I put down the food container and look him in the eye. "Not Valerie. She told me about adopting you."

"Yeah, I don't get it. I'm seventeen; I don't need anyone to take care of me."

"Maybe you're just scared Valerie's going to give up on you, too." He shrugs and turns away. "Maybe."

"I bet you a million bucks she won't." I touch his shoulder and say in a real serious voice, "And by the way, I'm not about to give up on you either." Then I grin and give him a swat. "Even though you're like the world's lamest opera singer."

"You . . . !" he shouts.

I dash away. He chases after me and swats me back. We're both laughing and breathing hard.

Then we stop and face each other, and I grin and start to give him a pretend shove in the chest, but he grabs my hand. He pushes his sunglasses to the top of his head. I find myself staring into his eyes.

"If I kissed you, would you run away again?"

My heart is pounding so hard I can't answer. He lets go of my hand and puts his big old arms around me. My cheek squashes against his chest, and we stand there like that for a minute. I breathe in his clean shower smell as he walks me backward until I press against the aviary fence; the wire mesh digs into my back. Then I slowly lift my chin while his lips come toward mine.

A car honks and we force ourselves apart. It's Valerie, pulling her little silver Honda into the driveway.

"Hey!" she calls out her window. "I could use some strong arms!"

I look into Alan's eyes and squeeze his hand.

"Got it!" he shouts back. We both go out to help her.

She has at least five bags of stuff in the trunk.

"I stocked up on supplies. Ferret chow was on sale, so I snagged twenty pounds. Got a good deal on mealworms, too."

The three of us lug the stuff into the cage room. Valerie crouches and opens a cupboard underneath the counter. "Let's stick them in here."

It takes a few minutes to figure out how to get everything into the already jammed cupboard. Finally Valerie straightens up, brushes her beige knit pants, and says, "There. We should be fine as long as we don't ever have to open it again." She laughs and puts her hands on her hips and smiles at me. "We don't see you for weeks, then you show up just when I need you most. Where have you been keeping yourself?"

I tell her about Mom coming back and about us staying at Tina's. "I really missed you guys," I say. "And Tweety Bird. And I've been wondering how that crow's doing."

She and Alan exchange a look, and he heads for the other part of the house.

"Oh, sweetheart," she says once he's gone, "I'm sorry to tell you this, but the crow didn't make it."

"It died?"

"I had to euthanize it."

"You killed it?"

"It's a very humane process." She puts her hand on my arm. "I'm sure it didn't feel a thing."

I jerk away. "You could have at least given it another week."

"A week wouldn't have made any difference. I knew the day you brought it in, that crow never had a chance."

I can't believe what I'm hearing. I always thought you were supposed to keep trying, keep hoping, no matter what. Anger surges through me. "How could you just give up?"

"I did what I could."

"You help all the other birds. Why didn't you save that one?"

"Honey, I wish you'd understand. Some birds can't be saved."

Her words rip into the very center of me. "No!" I flap and flail, sending trays and syringes clattering to the floor. "No! No!"

Then her arms surround me. I jerk and twist, but she doesn't let go. I'm surprised how strong she is. "It's okay," she whispers. "You're safe."

I struggle again, but she's holding me tight.

"Shhhh."

One last flutter and I give in. I put my arms around her and lay my head on her chest. It feels good to stop trying so hard. It feels good to finally let go.

At first it's little things. Mom starts sleeping late; I tell myself she's tired. Every once in a while she sniffles and swipes at her nose; I figure she must be catching a cold. When she gets up in the afternoon all cranky and mean, I decide it's because she's still adjusting to being home.

Aunt Mindy keeps leaving me messages about registering for Ballard High, but I delete them all. I can't think about school right now. In fact, the only thing I really want to think about is Alan.

We've been spending a lot of time together the last couple of weeks, and not just feeding birds. One afternoon when we were done at On the Wing, we grabbed some burgers at Dick's and had a picnic at the Overlook. Another night he took me to this all-ages club to see his friend's band. We've kissed a few times too, but never like that one time in the aviaries. I always get the feeling he's holding something back.

One Friday night in the middle of August, Valerie invites me over for dinner, and afterward the three of us watch a movie. Alan sits close to me on the couch, and I'm so zeroed in on the spot where our legs touch that I can hardly keep track of the plot. Valerie's car is in the shop, so when the movie's over, Alan walks me to the bus stop. It's starting to rain, and it's around ten when I get off the bus at Northgate Way and head down Aurora toward Tina's. I've gone a couple of blocks when I notice a faded red pickup going in the opposite direction. When it stops at the light a few feet ahead of me, I freeze. I'd know that truck anywhere.

I shouldn't look inside, but I do. Sitting in the driver's seat, one hand on the wheel, the other running across his buzzcut, is Drake. And sitting beside him, talking and waving a cigarette, is Mom.

I try to look away, but I can't. Before I can decide what to do, the light changes. He guns the engine, and they're gone.

I run the rest of the way to Tina's, my heart fluttering in my chest like a bird's wings, and burst through the front door. I dash down to Mom's room and pull my heart-shaped box from under her bed.

The money Aunt Mindy gave me is still there.

I sink onto the bed, shaking. What's wrong with me? I promised I was going to trust her.

But how can I trust her when she's hanging out with Drake? I slam the box onto the floor and kick it under the bed. I'm the one who begged her to come home, who dragged her out of rehab. If she's back on meth, I've got no one but myself to blame.

But maybe there's a perfectly good reason she was in that truck. Maybe Tina's car broke down and she needed a ride to work and he was the only one she could call. The more I think about it, the more I'm sure that's what happened and she'll tell me all about it when she gets home.

I decide to wait up for her. To kill time, I clean the kitchen. Rain taps against the windows as I wash every dish, including Dave's greasy black wok. I take out the stinky garbage and scrape at the globs of hardened spaghetti sauce on the stovetop. I even get down on my hands and knees, grit my teeth, and scrub the grime off the floor. It takes hours, but at least it keeps me awake.

Not that that's a problem. The later it gets, the more wired I feel. At two in the morning I move on to the living room, where I use Tina's straggly broom to whack cobwebs off the ceiling.

I'm about to start in on the bathroom when I hear a car pull up outside. Car door slamming, laughter, key in the lock.

Mom.

She's wearing her work clothes: backless top, tight skirt, six-inch heels. Droplets of rain glitter in her hair. "Hey, baby," she says. "You still up?"

I let the broom clatter to the floor and throw my arms around her. I bury my face against her neck and breathe in her jasmine-and-cigarette smell.

She unwinds my arms, looks at me through bloodshot eyes, her pupils huge and dark, and laughs that big, husky laugh. "Well, hello to you too."

"I cleaned the place up." I take her hand. "Come see the kitchen."

"Look, sweetie, I don't have time right now. I'm going out."

"What? With who?"

She heads for the basement stairs. I follow.

"With who?" I ask again.

"Hang on a minute, okay?" She goes into her room and shuts the door.

"You needed a ride to work, right? That's why you called him."

There's a muffled sound of movement from behind the door.

"Mom?"

No answer.

"Mom! That's why you called him, right?"

The door opens. She's wearing the outfit Aunt Mindy bought me; her red bra strap peeks through the cut-out triangle. The way she fills out the top, it looks even better on her than it does on me.

"Huh?" she says.

"Drake. I saw you in his truck."

She brushes past me and hurries up the stairs.

I'm right behind her. "What were you doing in Drake's truck?"

"I wasn't in his damn truck, okay?"

"I just want to know, that's all."

"Would you give it a rest?"

"But I saw you. Stopped at a red light."

"I thought you were going to trust me." She swipes at her nose with the back of her hand and heads for the front door.

For a second I feel bad for letting her down; then I shake it off. I block her way. "You're going out with him right now, aren't you?"

She moves toward me, puts her hand on my arm. "Oh, Stevie, you got yourself worked up over nothing. Now why don't you get ready for bed, and we'll talk in the morning? I promise. We'll go out for breakfast and order French toast." She smiles and pats my cheek. "I know you love French toast, don't you, honey pie?"

Honey pie. I feel myself starting to crumble under the weight of her promises. It takes all my strength to pull away. "I don't want any French toast."

"Then what the hell *do* you want?"

Her question and the look on her face stop me in my tracks. What do I want? I want her to ask me if I've had dinner and whether I've done my homework and how was my day at school. I want her to hassle me about the future and am I going to go to college and what do I want to be when I grow up. I even want her to get on my case and tell me I better not drink or do drugs, or else. But most of all I want her to want to be with me.

"I want you to start acting like a real mom."

She stares at me and opens her mouth, then shuts it. A horn honks outside. She opens the front door a crack. "Hang on!" she calls.

She turns to me with tears in her eyes, and for a second I see the Mom from my dream.

"I wish I could do that, baby," she whispers. "I really wish I could." She opens the door wider.

"If you leave, I won't be here when you get back."

But she's already gone.

I hurtle down the front steps. "Mom!"

Drake's truck is idling at the curb, wipers sweeping the windshield. He pushes open the passenger door.

I grab at Mom's arm as she clambers in. "It's him or me!" I yell through my tears.

"Quit it, Stevie. Go," she tells him, and slams the door.

I pound against the side of the truck. "Him or me!" I scream.

Drake looks at me now and smiles. *I've got her,* his smile seems to say. *And one of these days, I'm going to get you too.*

The truck tires squeal as he pulls away.

I stare after them until they turn the corner, and then I run back into the house, down the stairs, into the basement. I pull my heart-shaped box from under Mom's bed.

This time it's empty.

I hurl the box across the room. When it hits the wall and cracks in two, I yell the worst words I can think of. I swear at Mom and I swear at Drake. But most of all, I swear at me. I should have made Mom stay in rehab, should have stayed home more, should have watched her closer, should have kept my stupid mouth shut . . .

In the middle of yelling and swearing and pounding on the bed, I stop.

And then I know: It wasn't Aunt Mindy messing with my mind, it was Mom. She was going to leave rehab whether I asked her to or not. She never wanted to be saved.

I go up to the living room and grab my cell. I dial the number. It rings once . . . twice . . . and then Aunt Mindy picks up.

"Stevie? Is everything all right?"

My voice cracks. "I need you to come get me."

My mind is empty and clear as I pack up my stuff: jeans, sweaters, swishy gypsy skirts. Tanks, camis, midriffs, bikinis. I start to throw in my plaid boxers, but I decide to leave them behind. They're not the kind of thing I wear anymore. Plus, I need to save room for my notebooks.

I can't really think about the future. I can't really think past this minute. But I'm going to need those notebooks if I decide to go back to school, if I decide to be an architect.

I haul my bag upstairs and then hold my breath and listen for Aunt Mindy's car.

CHAPTER 20

When Aunt Mindy pulls up, I snatch my bag and fling the front door open before she even has a chance to knock. "Let's go," I say.

She doesn't ask questions. She pops her trunk and tosses my bag inside. The Smooth Jazz station plays as we drive. The music is so corny I could puke, but I don't complain. I stare out the window at the street, shiny wet under the streetlights, and the dark shapes of houses and trees.

"I'll make us some tea," she says once we get to the house. I go to stash my stuff in the guest room. My room. The bed is all made up, waiting for me, and everything smells clean and fresh.

I prop myself against a pillow, and she hands me a steaming mug of peppermint tea. The first sip burns my tongue. I take a second sip, then drink it down in big, scorching gulps.

Aunt Mindy watches me from the foot of the bed. She's thrown a purple bathrobe over her clothes.

"You ready to tell me what happened?"

I wrap my arms around my knees and scrunch up tight. "Mom's using again."

"How do you know? Are you sure?"

"She took off with Drake. And the hundred bucks you gave me is gone."

"Could one of your housemates have taken it? Or—"

"She's been staying up all night again. She's acting weird and her nose runs and . . ." I'm shaking so hard, I can't finish my sentence.

"Oh, sweetie, you're shivering. Let me get something to warm you up." She hurries out of the room and comes back with a blanket.

It is soft and white, with blue flowers. She tucks it around my legs and feet.

A new memory strikes me. It's so strong that I can't speak. I'm a little girl again, seeing a kind face hovering over me, feeling the warm weight of the blanket on my body.

I sit up, push it off me. I feel myself slipping, falling, not wanting to believe what my heart knows is true. "You took this blanket from Mom."

"No, your grandma gave it to me a long time ago." She makes me lie back and smoothes it over me again.

"Then Mom must have had one just like it."

"I don't think so. She wouldn't even touch it. She was always jealous your grandma gave this one to me, and she got the plaid one."

I shake my head. "She cuddled me in this blanket once a long time ago. She told me not to worry and that she'd take care of me."

Aunt Mindy's voice is soft. "You remember that?"

I nod and trace a blue flower with my finger, still hanging on to the hope that the memory was about Mom.

She catches hold of my hand. Tears shine in her eyes. "When you were really young—two, three maybe—your mom took off. We were living together then, sharing an apartment. This was back when we all lived in Helena. I woke up one morning and she was gone. No note, no phone call. Nothing. I was so scared. I thought something terrible must have happened to her."

I feel cold, colder than I've ever been in my life. I pull the blanket tight around me.

"I didn't know the first thing about looking after a little kid. I was trying to figure out who I could get to take care of you, thought maybe I could bring you up to Uncle Rob's for a while. Then you woke up and started crying for your mom. And when I saw your sweet face all screwed up tight, looking so lost and scared, I knew I couldn't pass you off on anyone else. That's when I got the blanket out of the cupboard and wrapped you up in it. I knew you loved those pretty blue flowers." She lays her other hand on top of mine. "And that's the day I decided that no matter what, I'd always be there for you."

I'm afraid I'll fall apart if I look at her. The blue flowers on the blanket blur. "But she came back," I whisper.

"Yes, she came back. Six months later. It's probably silly, but I'd started to think of you as my own. Then she showed up, said she'd found a job in Billings and wanted to take you with her. I wished so much I could hold on, but I had to let you go. After all, you were her little girl." Aunt Mindy drags the heel of her hand across her cheek, wiping away the tears. "When the chance came up to open the studio in Seattle, I took it. I had no idea that ten years later, when June ran out of options, she'd follow me here." She touches my cheek. "But I'm glad she did."

The past years with Mom rush back at me. All the times it was just me and her whooping and dancing and dreaming about the future. All the times we had to pick up and move, the schools I had to leave, the friends I had to say goodbye to. All the cramped, ugly apartments, the greasy, cardboard meals, the thrift-store clothes. All the nights I spent alone.

"I'm never going back." I throw myself onto Aunt Mindy's lap and bawl and bawl. She holds me and strokes my hair. When there are no more tears, I lie there, trying to take in a quiet breath.

She leans over me and whispers in my ear. "Don't worry, Stevie. Everything is going to be okay."

Two weeks later, the day before school starts, Aunt Mindy takes me shopping at Northgate Mall. I pick out a few pairs of jeans, some T-shirts and skirts, a couple of sweaters. Nothing fancy, just regular stuff. For once I want to look like everybody else. Well, okay, like everybody else who's got black nail polish, a belly button ring, and a Tweety Bird tattoo. Aunt Mindy was fine with the tattoo as long as it's in a place I can cover up. Which it is, unless I'm wearing a bikini. Or low-rise jeans and a midriff.

On the way out of the mall, we pass Victoria's Secret. The mannequin in the window is wearing a super-low-cut black lace tank and a short leather skirt. Her hip juts out to one side, and her head's thrown back like she's laughing. She looks so real—and so much like Mom—I have to swallow back the lump in my throat.

"Come on, Stevie," Aunt Mindy calls. "I've got to get back to the studio."

I look again. This time I see nothing but a woman made of plastic. "Coming," I say.

Aunt Mindy and I talked about me going back to Ballard High, but I decided on Nathan Hale, which is right in her neighborhood. I walk the halls in my jeans and sweaters and no one knows me. No one whispers about Mom. After all the school I missed last spring, I thought for sure I'd be way behind. But thanks to Rick, math actually seems easy.

When I see the notice in the *Daily Bulletin* about the Architecture Club, I think, *Me, in a club?* But Rick said to take myself seriously. And an Architecture Club sounds pretty serious. So one Thursday after school, I show up at Room 318.

When I open the door, about twenty guys stare back at me. I never thought of architecture as a guy thing, but obviously it is. Then a hand pops up above the sea of baseball-cap-covered heads.

"Over here." The hand waves, making silver bracelets jangle.

I slide into the seat next to the only other girl in the room.

"Hi," I say. "My name's Stevie."

Even though Aunt Mindy thinks I should focus on school, I'm not about to stop volunteering at On the Wing. Every weekend I take an early bus to help Alan with the first feeding.

One rainy Saturday at the end of September, I walk into the cage room to find him behind the counter, cutting up salmon-berries. His dark hair falls over his face, hiding his eyes.

"Hey," he says without looking up.

"Hey, yourself." I hang my raincoat by the door and slide around to his side of the counter. "Need any help?"

"Not really," he says, but he hands me a knife.

Neither of us is big on early morning conversation. For a couple of minutes the only sound in the room is the rhythmic *chop, chop, chop* of our knives on the cutting board. The berry juice stains my fingers yellowish-orange, and the tart smell tickles my nostrils. When we reach for a berry at the same time and our hands touch, I shoot him a smile.

"Who are these for?" I ask.

"The cedar waxwings. We just moved them to the aviary."

We chop for another minute or two, then he says, "That should be enough." He mixes the berry pieces with some dry food, loads up a feeding tray, and puts on his sunglasses. "I'm going to take these out back."

He doesn't ask me to come along, but I do anyway. The rain has stopped, and the sun peeks through the clouds, making the wet grass sparkle. When we let ourselves into the first aviary, the birds greet us with their usual chirps and caws. Tweety Bird perches on a branch and tilts her head, watching us through beady eyes.

"So, how's the school thing going?" Alan asks as he sets the bowl of dry food on the aviary floor. A jay swoops down and starts to peck at it.

"It's okay. You're lucky you don't have to go."

"Yeah, I guess." He empties the water dish and refills it. "I kind of wish I was, though."

"You're kidding me, right?"

He laughs. "Yeah, I know, it sounds lame. The thing is, the birds are great, but . . ."

"But what?"

"Well, I guess I miss being around people."

"So why don't you go back to school?"

"Valerie wants me to, but . . . I don't know. There's no way I could face going back to Ballard High. Not after what happened with Jeff Taylor."

He's never talked about it before, but I try not to show I'm surprised. "Yeah, I heard about that."

"Well, I had to do something after the crap he pulled on me," he says. Then his body tenses up, and he gets that don't-mess-with-me look in his eyes. He transforms into the old Alan right in front of me.

I don't really know Jeff Taylor, but he always seemed like an all-around nice guy.

He must see the question on my face, because he says, "Yeah, I know. Jeff's great. Until you have to live with him."

"Wait a second. You lived with Jeff Taylor?"

He fills a syringe and lures a crow off its branch. "Yep. Foster family number eight. The Taylors probably thought taking in a foster kid would fast-track them into heaven." He's leaning over the crow, so I can't see his face. "Little Prince Jeff wasn't so hot on the idea, though."

He finishes feeding the crow, then puts down the syringe and peels off his latex gloves. "He started doing stupid crap—swiping my stuff, breaking things around the house and blaming it on me. Mostly I ignored it. But then he . . ." He swears under his breath and turns away.

It takes him a minute to calm down, but he finally tells me the story: How Jeff found the photo of Alan's mom, the one he always kept under his pillow. How he said she looked like a whore and then ripped it into little pieces. How Alan had found the *Playgirl* magazines jammed behind Jeff's dresser and knew exactly how to get back at him.

When he's done, he takes a deep breath. "It was the only picture I had of her." He looks at me, and his voice breaks. "If I'd known he'd . . . that he'd end up in the hospital, I never would have done it. I tried to visit him, tell him I was sorry, but they wouldn't let me in."

I watch him gather up the feeding supplies. I still don't like what he did to Jeff, but at least I can halfway understand it. He's about to unlatch the door of the second aviary when I put my hand on his arm.

"You should go to Nathan Hale. My aunt could probably help get you in."

"I don't know." He won't look at me. He lets himself into the aviary and sets down the feeding tray.

I follow him inside. "It would be so awesome. We'd see each other every day."

"I'd be like the world's oldest eleventh-grader. People would think I'm a retard or something."

"No way. They'd think you're cool."

"Yeah, right."

"I'm serious. I mean, you're smart and funny and . . ."

Finally he cracks a smile. He slides his sunglasses to the top of his head. "And? Go on."

I punch him in the shoulder. "Fish for compliments, why don't you?"

"Hey, I almost forgot. This is for you."

He reaches into his pocket and gives me a square wooden box that fits perfectly in the palm of my hand. "Tweety Bird" is carved into the lid.

I breathe in the smell of fresh wood and then run my finger over the rough letters. "You made this?"

"I thought you'd want something to remember your robin by. Go ahead, open it."

I slide off the lid. A single gray-brown feather nestles inside.

I take it out and brush it against my cheek. "Thanks." I know I'm going to keep the box, and Tweety Bird's feather, forever.

Alan's eyes are deep and dark, and I feel like I could gaze into them forever. But his lips are closing in on mine, so I shut my eyes, and we kiss long and soft and slow, birds chirping in the background.

On a Sunday afternoon two weeks later, Valerie, Alan, and I pile into Valerie's car. In the trunk is a big cardboard box, and in that box is Tweety Bird.

"This is the place," Valerie says, and she pulls into a small gravel parking lot at the north end of the Arboretum. Aunt Mindy and

Rick, who've been following us in his Maserati, pull up next to us. We step into a scene that looks like a postcard. The rolling lawns of the Arboretum are deep green, but the leaves on the trees have turned brown and gold. A blue sky stretches over gray water, and above it all, the mountains show off a dusting of white snow. The air smells sharp and fresh.

"Stevie tells me she found this robin near the Crown Hill Cemetery," Rick says as he helps Valerie unload the box from the back of the car and set it on the grass. "Why are we releasing it here instead of back where she found it?"

"Lots of flocks pass through here on their way south," Valerie says. "We're hoping this robin will join one."

Aunt Mindy hooks her arm through Rick's. "That makes sense."

Honking fills the air as a flock of geese flies overhead. They head out across the water and the whole flock turns, never breaking their V-formation. It's like they've got some computer chip inside, telling them exactly what to do.

Alan hasn't said much all morning, but when I glance his way, I catch him staring at me. I'm glad I wore one of my new pairs of jeans and my favorite baby blue sweater. He motions me to the box.

"You want to do the honors?"

He makes it sound so simple, but I can hardly imagine opening that box and setting Tweety Bird free.

"Why don't we do it together?" Valerie says.

We squat near the box. Alan, Valerie, and I take the corners; Rick and Aunt Mindy find a spot on one side. Rick grabs the lid and slides his other arm around Aunt Mindy's waist. It's crowded, but I can't help feeling there's someone missing.

"On the count of three," Alan says. "One . . ."

Even though the morning is chilly, I break out in a sweat. What if Tweety Bird doesn't know what to do? She'll probably sit in the bottom of the box till we force her out.

"Two . . ."

I look up. Alan's brown eyes reflect the gold of the leaves. He says the last number right to me.

"Three!"

The second we lift the lid, Tweety Bird flits away and lands in the tree right next to us. She preens her feathers with her beak and cocks her head from side to side.

"How long is she going to stay there?" I ask.

"Shhh," Alan says. "Watch."

With a loud chirp, she flaps her wings and lifts right off the branch. She seems to hover in the air for a second, then she swoops over us and glides toward the water.

Rick and Aunt Mindy cheer; Valerie claps her hands. I want to cheer too, but the lump in my throat won't let me.

Aunt Mindy's eyes catch mine, and she comes up beside me and gives me a squeeze. I lean my head against her shoulder. Alan grabs my hand, and I hang on tight. We watch till the robin's just a speck in the wide blue sky.

ACKNOWLEDGMENTS

Thank you to my wonderful agent, Chris Richman of Upstart Crow Literary, for taking a chance on me and giving my story wings. Thanks also to my brilliant editor, Samantha McFerrin, for attending to every detail, and to everyone at Houghton Mifflin Harcourt who helped *Flyaway* soar.

I am grateful to Candy Brown, Rebecca Mandell, and the staff at PAWS Wildlife Rehabilitation Center in Lynwood, Washington, for teaching me about bird care and giving me firsthand experience in feeding wild birds, and to Shirley Shumway of Second Chance Wildlife Care Center in Snohomish, Washington, for allowing me a peek into a home-based wildlife rehabilitation clinic. Thank you, as well, to D'Artagnan Caliman for sharing his expertise in and experience with the foster care system.

A special thanks to Darcy Pattison, whose excellent Novel Revision Retreat gave me the tools to transform my rough draft into a viable novel, and to all the members of my critique group, past and present, whose feedback guided me in honing my words.

Last, but certainly not least, I will be forever indebted to my husband, Steven Bishofsky, for always being there with an encouraging word and a listening ear, and to my parents, Bernard and Gloria Rimland, for giving me the courage to chase my dreams.